SAPPHIRE

Sapphire is the author of the *New York Times* bestselling novel *The Kid*. She is also the author two books of poetry, *American Dreams* and *Black Wings & Blind Angels*. Her novel *Push* spent thirteen weeks in the number one position on the *New York Times* Bestseller List and was nominated for an NAACP Image Award in the category of Outstanding Literary Fiction. In 2009 *Push* was made into the Academy Award winning movie 'Precious' described by *Rolling Stone Magazine* as the Best Picture of 2009.

Sapphire's poetry and prose has been published in numerous journals and magazines including *The New Yorker*, *Black Scholar*, *PN Review*, *Spin*, and *BOMB*. Sapphire's work has been translated into fourteen languages and adapted for stage in North America, Europe and Africa.

Sapphire lives in New York City where she is working on a new novel and a selected volume of her poetry.

SAPPHIRE

Push

PREFACE BY
Tayari Jones

AFTERWORD BY
Sapphire

VINTAGE

Vintage is part of the Penguin Random House group of companies
whose addresses can be found at global.penguinrandomhouse.com

Penguin
Random House
UK

Copyright © Sapphire / Romona Lofton 1996

Sapphire / Romona Lofton has asserted her right to be identified as
the author of this Work in accordance with the Copyright, Designs
and Patents Act 1988

Preface copyright © 2021 by Tayari Jones
Afterword copyright © 2021 by Sapphire/Ramona Lofton

Grateful acknowledgement is made to Alfred A. Knopf, Inc. for
permission to reprint 'Mother and Son' from *Selected Poems* by
Langston Hughes, © 1926 by Alfred A. Knopt Inc, copyright re-
newed 1954 by Langston Hughes

This Vintage Classics edition first published in 2021
First published in Vintage in 1998
Also published by Vintage in 2010 as *Precious*
First published in Great Britain by Secker & Warburg in 1996

penguin.co.uk/vintage

A CIP catalogue record for this book is available
from the British Library

ISBN 9781784877361

Printed and bound in Italy by Grafica Veneta S.p.A.

The authorised representative in the EEA is Penguin Random House
Ireland, Morrison Chambers, 32 Nassau Street, Dublin D02 YH68

Penguin Random House is committed to a sustainable future
for our business, our readers and our planet. This book is
made from Forest Stewardship Council® certified paper.

MIX
Paper from
responsible sources
FSC® C018179

For children everywhere.
And for my teachers Eavan Boland,
James D. Merritt,
and most especially
Susan Fromberg Schaeffer.

If thou be one whose heart the holy forms
Of young imagination have kept pure,
Stranger! henceforth be warned; and know, that pride,
Howe'er disguised in its own majesty,
Is littleness; that he who feels contempt
For any living thing, hath faculties
Which he has never used; that thought with him
Is in its infancy. The man, whose eye
is ever on himself, doth look on one,
The least of nature's works, one who might move
The wise man to that scorn which wisdom holds
Unlawful, ever. O, be wiser thou!
Instructed that true knowledge leads to love . . .

WILLIAM WORDSWORTH

Every blade of grass has its Angel that bends over it
and whispers, "Grow, grow."

THE TALMUD

Preface

Tayari Jones

In the Reagan years, I was a teenager, more reader than writer, when I discovered the work of Sapphire. As a college student, I hung out with a cluster of intense artsy types, sharing battered copies of chapbooks, zines, and small-press volumes. My good friend Angela passed me a sheaf of xeroxed pages by an author who called herself Sapphire. What I remember most clearly was a persona poem from the point of view of Celestine Tate Harrington, the quadriplegic boardwalk singer who fought the city for custody of her child. The poem was defiant as the speaker focused less on the joys of motherhood and more on ownership of her sexuality. Angela speculated that Sapphire would likely never receive her due in the world of letters, because she had chosen as her subject the people whose bodies are stigmatized, whose families are pathologized, and whose very lives are held up as everything America rejects. "She is a hero," Angela declared, and I nodded in solemn agreement.

Imagine our shock and delight in 1996 when the entire literary world was on fire with the publication of *Push*—the author had been given a major advance, the first chapter would appear in *The New Yorker*, and there would be a serious book tour. I called Angela, as we were now living on opposite sides of the country, trying to figure out adult life. "Is that *our* Sapphire?" This was pre-internet, so I ran to the bookstore. The slick packaging was a far cry from the tattered pages we'd passed back and forth, and the woman in the author photo wore a close crop instead of long thick dreadlocks, but the fingerprint of an author is her words.

Push is told in the extraordinary voice of Claireece Precious Jones, who introduces her story with an agonizing declaration: "I was left back when I was twelve because I had a baby for my fahver." From there unspools a novel that is a merciless indictment of a society that abandons its most vulnerable citizens.

Without a doubt, Precious has trouble a-plenty. In addition to being impregnated by her father twice, she is also raped and beaten by her mother. She is functionally illiterate, obese, and destitute. She lives at the intersection of racism, sexism, classism, colorism, and more. Yet while her life is certainly shaped by these forces, they do not compromise her vibrant humanity.

Push the novel is much like Precious herself. Some critics were appalled by the very idea of this story, with this heroine, being held up as an important work of literature—just as Precious herself, walking down the streets of Harlem, endures stares and sneers from people who resent the very fact of her existence. The response to this work was similar to that of *The Color*

Purple, with some of the same critics bitterly complaining that the novel failed to present Black men in a positive light. But this novel, like Precious herself, finds its people.

Precious's people are Ms. Rain, the teacher from Each One Teach One, the alternative school where Precious learns to read and, just as important, to write. There, she meets an unforgettable cadre of young women who create a community that heals their trauma and empowers them, both on the pages of their journals as well as in their day-to-day lives. *Push* is a heartbreaker and a heart mender in one.

Push's people are those who know firsthand the trouble Sapphire has seen. They are the survivors, the first responders, the essential workers, and the school teachers. They are also those who have never known the pain of homelessness, AIDS, or incest but who desire a world without these scourges.

A novel is a work of art, and *Push* is no exception. The miracle of Sapphire's gift is that she weaves her sharp social commentary and critique into the fabric of this story without shredding its fibers. This is a novel about people and their problems, not problems and their people. Sapphire the poet begat Precious, a poet in her own right. This book is like a crown of sonnets, each movement lending an image to the next, building upon itself, growing in beauty and intensity.

This is no easy read. It is accessible, but no, never easy. The experience of reading this novel is best cap-

PREFACE

tured in the scene when Precious gives birth on the kitchen floor, the scene from which the novel takes its name. As she is racked with labor pains, the EMT coaches, "When that shit hit you again, go with it and push, Preshecita. *Push*."

Sapphire wants us not to push *past* the pain, injustice, and trauma. Instead, we must push *through* it. We must feel it to be changed by it. By the last page, we don't have the type of happy ending that Precious would call a "*Color Purple*." Yet we have the gift of a new day and a mandate to act.

When I finished *Push* in 1996, I immediately called my college friend, breathless and clutching the slim book to my breast. "It's the same Sapphire. I can tell."

"Yeah," Angela sighed. "It's her. Always a hero."

PUSH

I was left back when I was twelve because I had a baby for my fahver. That was in 1983. I was out of school for a year. This gonna be my second baby. My daughter got Down Sinder. She's retarded. I had got left back in the second grade too, when I was seven, 'cause I couldn't read (and I still peed on myself). I should be in the eleventh grade, getting ready to go into the twelf' grade so I can gone 'n graduate. But I'm not. I'm in the ninfe grade.

I got suspended from school 'cause I'm pregnant which I don't think is fair. I ain' did nothin'!

My name is Claireece Precious Jones. I don't know why I'm telling you that. Guess 'cause I don't know how far I'm gonna go with this story, or whether it's even a story or why I'm talkin'; whether I'm gonna start from the beginning or right from here or two weeks from now. Two weeks from now? Sure you can do anything when you talking or writing, it's not like living when you can only do what you doing. Some people tell a story 'n it don't make no sense or be true. But I'm gonna try to make sense and tell the truth, else what's the fucking use? Ain' enough lies and shit out there already?

So, OK, it's Thursday, September twenty-four 1987 and I'm walking down the hall. I look good, smell good—fresh, clean. It's hot but I do not take off my leather jacket even though it's hot, it might get stolen or lost. Indian summer, Mr Wicher say. I don't know why he call it that. What he mean is, it's *hot*, 90 degrees, like summer days. And there is no, none, I mean *none*, air conditioning in this mutherfucking building. The building I'm talking about is, of course, I.S. 146 on 134th Street between Lenox Avenue and Adam Clayton Powell Jr Blvd. I am walking down the hall from home-room to first period maff. Why they put some shit like maff first period I do not know. Maybe to gone 'n git it over with. I actually don't mind maff as much as I had thought I would. I jus' fall in Mr Wicher's class sit down. We don't have assigned seats in Mr Wicher's class, we can sit anywhere we want. I sit in the same seat everyday, in the back, last row, next to the door. Even though I know that back door be locked. I don't say nuffin' to him. He don't say nuffin' to me, *now*. First day he say, "Class turn the book pages to page 122 please." I don't move. He say, "Miss Jones, I *said* turn the book pages to page 122." I say, "Mutherfucker I ain't deaf!" The whole class laugh. He turn red. He slam his han' down on the book and say, "Try to have some disci-pline." He a skinny little white man about five feets four inches. A peckerwood as my mother would say. I look at him 'n say, "I can slam too. You wanna slam?" 'N I pick up my book 'n slam it down on the desk hard. The class laugh some more. He say, "Miss Jones I would appreciate it if you would leave the room right NOW." I say, "I ain' going nowhere mutherfucker till the bell ring. I came here to learn maff and you gon' teach me." He look like a bitch just got a train pult on her. He don't know what to do. He try to recoup, be cool, say, "Well, if you want to learn, calm down—" "I'm calm," I tell him. He say, "If you want to learn, shut up and open your book." His face is red, he is shaking. I back off. I have won. I guess.

I didn't want to hurt him or embarrass him like that you know. But I couldn't let him, anybody, know, page 122 look like page 152, 22, 3, 6, 5—all the pages look alike to me. 'N I really do want to learn. Everyday I tell myself something gonna happen, some shit like on TV. I'm gonna break through or somebody gonna break through to me—I'm gonna learn, catch up, be normal, change my seat to the front of the class. But again, it has not been that day.

But thas the first day I'm telling you about. Today is not the first day and like I said I was on my way to maff class when Mrs Lichenstein snatch me out the hall to her office. I'm really mad 'cause actually I like maff even though I don't do nuffin', don't open my book even. I jus' sit there for fifty minutes. I don't cause trouble. In fac' some of the other natives get restless I break on 'em. I say, "Shut up mutherfuckers I'm tryin' to learn something." First they laugh like trying to pull me into fuckin' with Mr Wicher and disrupting the class. Then I get up 'n say, "Shut up mutherfuckers I'm tryin' to learn something." The coons clowning look confuse, Mr Wicher look confuse. But I'm big, five feet nine-ten, I weigh over two hundred pounds. Kids is scared of me. "Coon fool," I tell one kid done jumped up. "Sit down, stop ackin' silly." Mr Wicher look at me confuse but grateful. I'm like the polices for Mr Wicher. I keep law and order. I like him, I pretend he is my husband and we live together in Weschesser, wherever that is.

I can see by his eyes Mr Wicher like me too. I wish I could tell him about all the pages being the same but I can't. I'm getting pretty good grades. I usually do. I just wanna gone get the fuck out of I.S. 146 and go to high school and get my diploma.

Anyway I'm in Mrs Lichenstein's office. She's looking at me, I'm looking at her. I don't say nuffin'. Finally she say, "So Claireece, I see we're expecting a little visitor." But it's not like a question, she's telling me. I still don't say nuffin'. She staring at me, from behind her big wooden desk, she got her white bitch hands folded together on top her desk.

"Claireece."

Everybody call me Precious. I got three names— Claireece Precious Jones. Only mutherfuckers I hate call me Claireece.

"How old are you Claireece?"

White cunt box got my file on her desk. I see it. I ain't that late to lunch. Bitch know how old I am.

"Sixteen is ahh rather ahh"—she clear her throat—"*old* to still be in junior high school."

I still don't say nuffin'. She know so much let her ass do the talking.

"Come now, you are pregnant, aren't you Claireece?"

She asking now, a few seconds ago the hoe just *knew* what I was.

"Claireece?"

She tryin' to talk all gentle now and shit.

"Claireece, I'm talking to you."

I still don't say nuffin'. This hoe is keeping me from maff class. I like maff class. Mr Wicher like me in there, need me to keep those rowdy niggers in line. He nice, wear a dope suit *every* day. He do not come to school looking like some of these other nasty ass teachers.

"I don't want to miss no more of maff class," I tell stupid ass Mrs Lichenstein.

She look at me like I said I wanna suck a dog's dick or some shit. What's with this cunt bucket? (That's what my muver call women she don't like, cunt buckets. I kinda get it and I kinda don't get it, but I like the way it sounds so I say it too.)

I get up to go, Mrs Lichenstein ax me to please sit down, she not through with me yet. But I'm through with her, thas what she don't get.

"This is your *second* baby?" she says. I wonder what else it say in that file with my name on it. I hate her.

"I think we should have a parent-teacher conference Claireece—me, you, and your mom."

"For what?" I say. "I ain' done nuffin'. I doose my work. I ain' in no trouble. My grades is good."

Mrs Lichenstein look at me like I got three arms or a bad odor out my pussy or something.

What my muver gon' do I want to say. What is she gonna do? But I don't say that. I jus' say, "My muver is busy."

"Well maybe I could arrange to come to your house—" The look on my face musta hit her, which is what I was gonna do if she said one more word. Come to my house! Nosy ass white bitch! I don't think so! We don't be coming to your house in Weschesser or wherever the fuck you freaks live. Well I be damned, I done heard everything, white bitch wanna visit.

"Well then Claireece, I'm afraid I'm going to have to suspend you—"

"For what!"

"You're pregnant and—"

"You can't suspend me for being pregnant, I got rights!"

"Your attitude Claireece is one of total uncooperation—"

I reached over the desk. I was gonna yank her fat ass out that chair. She fell backwards trying to get away from me 'n started screaming, "SECURITY SECURITY!"

I was out the door and on the street and I could still hear her stupid ass screaming, "SECURITY SECURITY!"

"Precious!" That's my mother calling me.

I don't say nothin'. She been staring at my stomach. I know what's coming. I keep washing dishes. We had fried chicken, mashed potatoes, gravy, green beans, and Wonder bread for dinner. I don't know how many months pregnant I am. I don't wanna stand here 'n hear Mama call me slut. Holler 'n shout on me all day like she did the last time. Slut! Nasty ass tramp! What you been doin'! Who! Who! WHOoooo like owl in Walt Disney movie I seen one time. Whooo? Ya wanna know who—

"Claireece Precious Jones I'm talkin' to you!"

I still don't answer her. I was standing at this sink the last time I was pregnant when them pains hit, *wump!* Ahh wump! I never felt no shit like that before. Sweat was breaking out on my forehead, pain like fire was eating me up. I jus' standing there 'n pain hit me, then pain go sit down, then pain git up 'n hit me harder! 'N she standing there *screaming* at me, "Slut! Goddam slut! You fuckin' cow! I don't believe this, right under my nose. You been high tailing it round here." Pain hit me again, then *she* hit me. I'm on the floor groaning, "Mommy please, Mommy please, please Mommy! Mommy! Mommy! MOMMY!" Then she KICK me side of my face! "Whore! Whore!" she screamin'. Then Miz West live down the hall pounding on the door, hollering "Mary! Mary! What you doin'! You gonna kill that chile! She need help not no beating, is you crazy!"

Mama say, "She shoulda tole me she was pregnant!"

"Jezus Mary, you didn't know. *I* knew, the whole building knew. Are you crazy—"

"Don't tell me nothin' about my own chile—"

"Nine-one-one! Nine-one-one! Nine-one-one!" Miz West screamin' now. She call Mama a fool.

Pain walking on me now. Jus' stomping on me. I can't see hear, I jus' screamin', "Mommy! Mommy!"

Some mens, these ambulance mens, I don't see 'em or hear 'em come in. But I look up from the pain and he dere. This Spanish guy in EMS uniform. He push me back on a cushion. I'm like in a ball from the pain. He say, "RELAX!" The pain stabbing me wif a knife and this spic talking 'bout relax.

He touch my forehead put his other hand on the side of my belly. "What's your name?" he say. "Huh?" I say. "Your name?" "Precious," I say. He say, "Precious, it's almost here. I want you to push, you hear me momi, when that shit hit you again, go with it and push, Preshecita. *Push*."

And I did.

And always after that I look for someone with his face and eyes in Spanish peoples. He coffee-cream color, good hair. I remember that. God. I think he was god.

No man was never nice like that to me before. I ask at the hospital behind him, "Where that guy help me?" They say, "Hush girl you jus' had a baby."

But I can't hush 'cause they keep asking me questions. My name? Precious Jones. Claireece Precious Jones to be exact. Birth date? November 4, 1970. Where? "*Here*," I say, "right chere in Harlem Hospital." "*Nineteen seventy?*" the nurse say confuse quiet. Then she say, "How old are you?" I say, "Twelve." I was heavy at twelve too, nobody get I'm twelve 'less I tell them. I'm tall. I jus' know I'm over two hundred 'cause the needle on the scale in the bathroom stop there it don't can go no further. Last time they want to weigh me at school I say no. Why for, I know I'm fat. So what. Next topic for the day.

But this not school nurse now, this Harlem Hospital where I was borned, where me and my baby got tooked after it was borned on the kitchen floor at 444 Lenox Avenue. This nurse slim butter-color woman. She lighter than some Spanish womens but I know she black. I can tell. It's something about being a nigger ain't color. This nurse same as me. A lot of black people with nurse cap or big car or light skin same as me but don't know it. I'm so tired I jus' want to disappear. I wish Miss Butter would leave me alone but she jus' staring at me, her eyes getting bigger and bigger. She say she need to get some more information for the birth certificate.

It still tripping me out that I had a baby. I mean I knew I was pregnant, knew how I got pregnant. I been knowing a man put his dick in you, gush white stuff in your booty you could get pregnant. I'm twelve now, I been knowing about that since I was five or six, maybe I always known about pussy and dick. I can't remember not knowing. No, I can't remember a time I did not know. But thas all I knowed. I didn't know how long it take, what's happening inside, nothing, I didn't know nothing.

The nurse is saying something I don't hear. I hear kids at school. Boy say I'm laffing ugly. He say, "Claireece is so ugly she laffing ugly." His fren' say, "No, that fat bitch is crying ugly." Laff laff. Why I'm thinking about those stupid boys now I don't know.

"Mother," she say. "What's your mother's name?" I say, "Mary L Johnston" (*L* for Lee but my mother don't like Lee, soun' too country). "Where your mother born," she say. I say, "Greenwood, Mississippi." Nurse say, "You ever been there?" I say, "Naw, I never been nowhere." She say, "Reason I ask is I'm from Greenwood, Mississippi, myself." I say, "Oh," 'cause I know I'm spozed to say something.

"Father," she say. "What's your daddy's name?"

"Carl Kenwood Jones, born in the Bronx."

She say, "What's the baby's father's name?"

I say, "Carl Kenwood Jones, born in the same Bronx."

She quiet quiet. Say, "Shame, thas a shame. Twelve years old, twelve years old," she say over 'n over like she crazy (or in some shock or something). She look at me, butter skin, light eyes—I know boyz love her. She say, "Was you ever, I mean did you ever get to be a chile?" Thas a stupid question, did I ever get to be a chile? I *am* a chile.

I'm confuse, tired. I tell her I want to sleep. She put the bed down, I do go to sleep.

Somebody else there when I wake up. It's like the police or something. Wanna ax me some questions. I axes, "Where's my baby? I know I had one. I know that." New somebody in nurse cap sweet-smile me and say, "Yes, you did Miss Jones, you surely did." She moves the men in uniform suits back from my bed. Say my baby is in special intense care and I will get to see her soon and won't I please answer the nice men's questions. But they ain' nice men. They pigs. I ain' crazy. I don't tell them nothing.

"Precious! Precious!" my muver hollering but my head not here, it in four years ago when I had the first baby. I was standing at this sink when the pain hit me, and she hit me.

"Precious!"

My hand slip down in the dishwater, grab the butcher knife. She bedda not hit me, I ain' lyin'! If she hit me I will stab her ass to def, you hear me!

"Precious! You done lost your mind? Just standing up there staring into spaces. I'm talkin' to you!"

Like thas something.

"I was thinkin'," I say.

"You thinkin' while I'm talkin' to you?"

She say this like I'm burnin' hunnert dollar bills.

The buzzer ring. I wonder who it could be. Don't nobody ring our bell 'less it's crack addicts trying to get in the building. I hate crack addicts. They give the race a bad name.

"Go tell them assholes to stop ringing the bell," she say. She closer to the door than me but I mean my muver don't move 'less she has to. I mean that. When I go to answer the buzzer I realize I'm still grabbing the knife. I hate my muver sometimes. She is ugly I think sometime.

I press TALK on the intercom and holler, "Stop ringing the goddam buzzer mutherfucker!" and go back to the kitchen to finish the dishes.

The buzzer ring again. I go back. "Stop ringing the goddam buzzer," I say again. The mutherfucker ring again. "Stop it!" It ring *again*. "STOP IT!" I shout again. It ring again. My muver jump in and say, "Press LISTEN stupid!" I wanna say I ain' stupid but I know I am so I don't say nothin', 'cause also I don't want her to go hit me, 'cause I know from my hand in the dishwater holding the butcher knife, I am through being hit. I am going to stab her she ever hit Precious Jones again. I press LISTEN. "It's Sondra Lichenstein for Claireece Jones and Ms Mary Johnston." *Mrs Lichenstein!* What that hoe want? She want me to hit her for real this time.

"Who that Precious?" my muver say. I say, "White bitch from school." "What she want?" my muver say. "I don't know." "Ask her," my muver say. I press TALK 'n say, "What you want?" Then I press LISTEN and Mrs Lichenstein say, "I want to talk to you about your education." This bitch crazy. I was going to school everyday till her honky ass snatch me out the hall, fuck with my mind, make me go off on her, suspend me from school jus' because I'm pregnant—you know, *end up* my education. Now her white ass out on Lenox Avenue talkin' 'bout she wanna talk to me about my education. Lord where is crack addicts when you need 'em. "What all this about Precious?" my muver asks. My muver don't want no white shit like Mrs Lichenstein social worker teacher ass nosing around here. My muver don't want to get cut off, welfare that is. And that's what white shit like Mrs Lichenstein comin' to visit result in. If I wasn't pregnant and having trouble with the stairs, I run down and kick her ass. My muver say, "Eighty-six that bitch." I says into the intercom, "Hasta la vista, baby." That's Spanish for good-bye but when niggers say it, it's like, kiss my ass. Ring go buzzer again. I don't believe this retarded hoe. I press TALK 'n say, "Git outta here Mrs Lichenstein 'fore I kick your ass." The bell go ring. I press LISTEN. "Claireece I am so sorry about Thursday. I had only wanted to help you. I . . . Mr Wicher says you're one of his best students, that you have an aptitude for math." She pause like she thinking what to say next, then she say, "I've called a Ms McKnight at Higher Education Alternative/Each One Teach One. It's an alternative school." She pause again, say, "Claireece, are you listening?" I press TALK. "Yeah," I say. "OK, as I was saying I've called Ms McKnight at Each One Teach One. It's located on the nineteenth floor of the Hotel Theresa on 125th Street. That's not too far from here." I press TALK. "I know where the Hotel Theresa is," I say to her, Bitch, I say to myself. I press LISTEN again, these crackers think you don't know nothin'. She say, "The phone number is 555-0831. I told them about you." Mrs Lichenstein stop. "Call or just drop in, the nineteenth floor—" I press TALK tell her I heard her the first time. My heart is all warm— half of it at least—thinking about Mr Wicher say I'm a good student. The other half could jus' jump out my chest and kick Mrs Lichenstein's ass. No more rings—so I guess that mean she got the message.

I go to sleep thinking nineteenth floor Hotel Theresa, an alternative. I don't know what an alternative is but I feel I want to know. Nineteenth floor, that's the last words I think before I go to sleep. I dream I'm in an elevator that's going up up up so far I think I'm dying. The elevator open and it's the coffee-cream-colored man from Spanish talk land. I recognize him from when I was having my baby bleeding on the kitchen floor. He put his hand on my forehead again and whisper, "Push, Precious, you gonna hafta *push*."

I wake up remembering the last time I pushed. It was two whole days before they brought the baby to me, 'n I git to see what "a little trouble breathing" mean. I try to hold out my arms but I'm tired, more tired than I ever been in my life. Nurse Butter and this little black nurse is standing there by my bed. The black nurse holding the baby. Nurse Butter reach under the covers and take my hands. I ball 'em in fist. She rub her hands over my fist till I open them. Nurse Butter look other nurse in eye and the dark-skinned nurse go to hand me my baby but Butter jump up and take it from her.

"Something is wrong with your baby," Nurse Butter make talk like how pigeons talk, real soft, coo coo, "but she's alive. And she's yours." 'N she hand me baby. Baby's face is smashed flat like pancake, eyes is all slanted up like Koreans, tongue goin' in 'n out like some kinda snake.

"Mongoloid," other nurse say. Nurse Butter look hard at her.

"What happen?" I ax.

"Well, a lot of things," she say. "The doctor will talk in more depth with you, Ms Jones. It looks like your baby may have Down's syndrome and have suffered some oxygen deprivation at birth. Plus you're so young, things happen more to the very young—" She ax me, "Did you see a doctor at all while you were pregnant?"

I don't answer her nuffin', jus' hold out baby for her to take. Nurse Butter nod to little black nurse who take baby away. Nurse Butter hike herself up on side of the bed. She tryin' to hole me in her arms. I don't want that. She touch side of my face. "I'm so sorry, Ms Jones, so *so* sorry." I try to turn away from her Mississippi self but she *in* the bed now pulling my chest and shoulders into her arms. I can smell her lotion smell and Juicy Fruit gum breath. I feel warm kindness from her I never feel from Mama and I start to cry. A little at first, then on and on, *everything* hurt—between my legs, the black-blue on the side of my head where Mama kick me, but Butter don't see it and she squeezing me there. I crying for ugly baby, then I forget about ugly baby, I crying for me who no one never hold before. Daddy put his pee-pee smelling thing in my mouth, my pussy, but never hold me. I see me, first grade, pink dress dirty sperm stuffs on it. No one comb my hair. Second grade, third grade, fourth grade seem like one dark night. Carl is the night and I disappear in it. And the daytimes don't make no sense. Don't make sense talking, bouncing balls, filling in between dotted lines. Shape? Color? Who care whether purple shit a square or a circle, whether it purple or blue? What difference it make whether gingerbread house on top or bottom of the page. I disappears from the day, I jus' put it all down— book, doll, jump rope, my head, myself. I don't think I look up again till EMS find me on floor, and now this little nurse telling me, "Look at me, sweetie, you gonna get through this. You really are gonna get through this."

I look at her but see Mama's shoe coming at the side of my head like a bullet, Carl's dick dangle dangle in my face and now the flat-face baby with eyes like Koreans.

"How," I ax her, "how?"

After I come home from hospital baby go live over on 150th and St Nicholas Avenue with my grandmother, even though Mama tell welfare the baby live with us and she care of it while I'm in school. About three months after baby born, I'm still twelve when all this happen, Mama slap me. HARD. Then she pick up cast-iron skillet, thank god it was no hot grease in it, and she hit me so hard on back I fall on floor. Then she kick me in ribs. Then she say, "Thank you Miz Claireece Precious Jones for fucking my husband you nasty little slut!" I feel like I'm gonna die, can't breathe, from where I have baby start to hurt.

"Fat cunt bucket slut! Nigger pig bitch! He done quit me! He done left me 'cause of you. What you tell them mutherfuckers at the damn hospital? I should KILL you!" she screaming at me.

I'm lying on the floor shaking, crying, scared she gonna kill me. "Get up Miss Hot-to-Trot," Mama say. "Git your Jezebel ass up and fix some dinner 'fore I give you something to cry about." So I get up from floor and fix dinner. I fix collard greens and ham hocks, corn bread, fried apple pies, and macaroni 'n cheese. I'm in the kitchen two hours, I know that, even though I don't tell time so good, 'cause man on the radio say four o'clock, tell some news, play music, and by the time I'm fixing Mama's plate man say six o'clock. My neck, shoulder, and back feel like cars is riding over them. I carry Mama a plate, set it in front her on TV tray.

"Where's yours?" Mama shout.

"I'm not hongry," I tell her.

Devil red sparks flashes in Mama's eyes, big crease in her forehead git deeper. I'm scared. "I . . . my shoulder hurt . . . I wanna lay down."

"Ain' nothin' wrong with your shoulder, I barely touched you! Go get a plate and stop acting stupid 'fore I do hurt your shoulder."

I go back to the kitchen and fix myself a plate. Mama holler, "Margarine! Bring me some margarine and hot sauce." So I bring her the margarine and the hot sauce. Then I go git my plate and sit down with her. Greens, corn bread, ham hocks, macaroni 'n cheese; I eat 'cause she say eat. I don't taste nothin'. The pain in my shoulder is throbbing me, shooting up my neck. Some white people is smiling and kissing on television. "Oh ain't he cute!" Mama going ape over black guy in beer commercial. I don't like beer. "Git me some more." Mama push her plate toward me. " 'N git you some more—"

"I don't want no more."

"Did you hear me?"

So I get up, take her and my plate to the kitchen. I'm so full I could bust. I look at Mama. Scare me to look at her. She take up half the couch, her arms seem like giant arms, her legs which she always got cocked open seem like ugly tree logs. I bring her plate back. "Ain' no more pies?"

"Yeah," I say.

"Bring me a few when you bring your plate back and hurry up 'fore I kick your stupid ass!"

So *back* to the kitchen, git her pies, pile my own plate higher than the first time, know if I don't she just gonna make me go back again. I sit her pies down on the tray. Try not to look at her. Try to watch the white people on TV running on the beach sand. Try not to see grease running down Mama's chin, try not to see her grab whole ham hock wif her hand, try not to see myself doing the same thing. Eating, first 'cause she make me, beat me if I don't, then eating hoping pain in my neck back go away. I keep eating till the pain, the gray TV light, and Mama is a blur; and I just fall back on the couch so full it like I'm dyin' and I go to sleep, like I always do; almost. *Almost*, go to sleep; it's the pain in my shoulder keep me from totally conking out this time. I feel Mama's hand between my legs, moving up my thigh. Her hand stop, she getting ready to pinch me if I move. I just lay still still, keep my eyes close. I can tell Mama's other hand between her legs now 'cause the smell fill room. Mama can't fit into bathtub no more. Go sleep, go sleep, go to *sleep*, I tells myself. Mama's hand creepy spider, up my legs, in my pussy. God please! Thank you god I say as I fall asleep.

I'm twelve, no I *was* twelve, when that shit happen. I'm sixteen now. For past couple of weeks or so, ever since white bitch Lichenstein kick me outta school shit, 1983 and 1987, twelve years old and sixteen years old, first baby and this one coming, all been getting mixed up in my head. Mama jus' hit me wif fryin' pan? Baby, brand-new and wrapped in white blankets, or fat and dead eyed lying in crib at my grandmother's house. Everything seem like clothes in washing machine at laundry mat—round 'n round, up 'n down. One minute Mama's foot smashing into side of my head, next I'm jumping over desk on Mrs Lichenstein's ass.

But now, right *now*, I'm standing at the sink finishing the dishes. Mama sleep on couch. It's Friday, October sixteen, 1987. I got to get through Saturday and Sunday 'fore I get to Monday—the alternative.

"*School?*" Mama say. "Go down to welfare, school can't help you none, *now*." Lady at Lane Bryant on one-two-five call these leggings YELLOW NEON. I'm wearing them and my X sweatshirt. Put some Vaseline on my face, nuffin' I can do about my hair till I git some money to git my braids put back in. I look at my poster of Farrakhan on the wall. Amen Allah! Radio clock glowing red 8:30 a.m. Time to go!

Mama sleep. I be back before she wake up, back in time to clean up and fix breakfast for Mama. Why Mama never do anything? One time I ax her, when I get up from her knocking me down, she say, That's what you here for.

I is goin' down to the nineteenth floor of the Hotel Teresa to the all-tur-nah-TIVE! Reeboks, white! Better than Nikes? No, next shits I get be Nikes! Green leather jacket, keys. I is going, got my hand on the doorknob.

"Where you going?" Mama holler from her room.

Why ain' her fat ass sleep? I don't say nuffin'. Fuck her!

"You hear me talking to you!" I start undoing locks on the front door. It's four of 'em. "Precious!" Fuck you bitch. Ize gone. The staircase so skinny both sides of me touch some part of building when I'm going down the stairs. Maybe after I have baby I lose some weight. Maybe I get my own place.

When I step out in morning Lenox is jumping with cars, gypsy cabs, and buses. Delivery trucks is parked in front the supermarket and the McDonald's on corner of 132nd. Men, women, and kids waiting at bus stop to go to school and downtown to work. Wonder where they go to work? Where I gonna go to work, how I'm gonna get out HER house? I hate her. Come to 126th Street, across the street Sylvia's. I ain't got no money. African vendors out on street wif they stuff—leather purses and African clothes and earrings from cow' shells, stuff like that.

I'm walking slow slow now. No one say nuffin' to me now my belly big. No "Yo Big Mama" 'n "all dat meat and no potatoes" shit. I'm safe. Yeah, safe from dese fools on the street but am I safe from Carl Kenwood Jones? This is my second baby for my daddy, it gonna be retarded too?

This time I know Mama know. Umm hmmm, she know. She bring him to me. I ain' crazy, that stinky hoe give me to him. Probably thas' what he require to fuck her, some of me. Got to where he jus' come in my room any ole time, not jus' night. He climb on me. Shut up! he say. He slap my ass, You wide as the Mississippi, don't tell me a little bit of dick hurt you heifer. Git usta it, he laff, you *is* usta it. I fall back on bed, he fall right on top of me. Then I change stations, change *bodies*, I be dancing in videos! In movies! I be breaking, *fly*, jus' a dancing! Umm hmm heating up the stage at the Apollo for Doug E. Fresh or Al B. Shure. They love me! Say I'm one of the best dancers ain' no doubt of or about that!

"I'm gonna marry you," he be saying. Hurry up, nigger, shut up! He mess up dream talkin' 'n gruntin'. First he mess up my life fucking me, then he mess up the fucking talkin'. I wanna scream, Oh shut up! Nigger, how you gonna marry me and you is my daddy. I'm your daughter, fucking me illegal. But I keep my mouf shut so's the fucking don't turn into a beating. I start to feel good; stop being a video dancer and start coming. I try to go back to video but coming now, rocking under Carl now, my twat jumping juicy, it feel good. I feel shamed. "*See, see*," he slap my thigh like cowboys do horses on TV, then he squeeze my nipple, bite down on it. I come some more. "*See*, you LIKE it! You jus' like your mama—you die for it!" He pull his dick out, the white cum stuff pour out my hole wet up the sheets.

"Are you getting on the bus, young lady?" I blink at bus driver staring down at me. He shake his head, bus door close. I'm leaning against glass panel of bus stop. I stare at 101 bus disappearing down 125th Street. How I git here? What I'm doing on one-two-five at this time of morning? I look down at my feet, my eyes catch on my leggings, NEON YELLOW, of course! Alternative! I'm on my way, *was* on my way, walking down Lenox when bad thoughts hit me 'n I space out.

"You OK?" guy in a uniform for like working in a garage ax me.

"I'm OK, I'm OK." People done started to gather 'round me.

"That bitch crazy man!" a skinny dude in baggies say real loud to tall boy next to him.

"Fuck you narrow behind mutherfucker! Mind your bizness!" I break out from them, cross 125th Street, and head for Hotel Theresa. I done passed it a hunnert times but never been in it. I walk through the doors, past man at desk, he don't say nuffin' to me, I don't say nuffin' to him. It's a elevator wif black doors. I step inside, stand there. Don't go nowhere. Push the button, stupid, I tell myself. I push the button; I'm not stupid, I tell myself.

I step out the elevator and see this lady with cornrow hair sitting at desk. White sign black letters on the desk.

"This the alternative?" I ax.

"The *what*?" She lift eyebrows.

"This the alternative?" That bitch heard me the first time!

"What exactly are you looking for?" woman nice talk.

"Well, what is this here?"

"This is Higher Education Alternative/Each One Teach One."

"I'm looking for alternative school."

"Well," woman look at me some more, "this *is* an alternative school."

I never seen nobody wif braids that don't hang down. Why git 'em put in if you not gonna get extensions.

"What alternative is?" Mayest wellst gone ask the bitch, fine out now what kinda school this gonna be.

"I don't know if I understand what you're asking me?"

"Alternative—lady from my other school tell me to come here to Hotel Theresa, nineteenth floor, it's 'alternative' school."

"OK, OK," she say, "Each One Teach One is an alternative school and an alternative is like a choice, a different way to do something."

"Oh."

"What school did you come from?"

"From I.S. 146."

"That's a junior high school, isn't it?"

"I'm sixteen."

"You need discharge papers from your old school saying they have formally discharged you or we can't allow you in the program."

"I got kicked out 'cause I was pregnant—"

"Yes, yes, I understand but you still need formal discharge papers or we can't let you in. It's the law."

"Mrs Lichenstein ain' say all that."

"Oh you're the one Mrs Lichenstein called about."

"What she say?"

She answer like she talking to herself, "Said to be on the lookout for you, you might be coming our way." She fumble with some papers on her desk. "Are you Claireece P. Jones?"

"Thas' me." So they was really on the lookout for me? Thas' kinda nice.

"Well the principal at I.S. 146 already sent your discharge papers and stuff over."

"What stuff?"

"Your academic record—" The woman stop stare at me. "Are you all right?"

"They done sent my file!" I almost spit it, it make me so mad.

"Well, we had to have ahh certain information before we could accept you into the program. Our students have to meet certain income, residential, and academic requirements before we can let them in the program. So really their sending your records over was just a way of speeding things up for you."

I wonder what exactly do file say. I know it say I got a baby. Do it say who Daddy? What kinda baby? Do it say how pages the same for me, how much I weigh, fights I done had? I don't know what file say. I do know every time they wants to fuck wif me or decide something in my life, here they come wif the mutherfucking file. Well, OK, they got file, know every mutherfucking thing. So what's the big deal, let's get it on.

"Can I start today?"

Ol' Cornrows' eyebrows go up. "Well of course," she say, "I mean we have an entry procedure but most of that has actually been completed for you. The only thing we really need is income verification. Are you currently receiving AFDC?"

"No."

Eyebrows up again, she look down nose over glasses.

"My muver get AFDC for me and my daughter."

"Oh you've had amniocentesis?" She looking at my belly now.

"Huh?"

"You said your mother was receiving a check for you and your daughter?" She nod her head to my stomach.

"Not this baby! I got another one 'sides this coming."

"Oh, I see, so your mother has custody of you and your daughter, in other words you're on her 'budget.' "

"Umm hmm." This bitch ain' no dummy.

"OK, well I need a copy of your mother's budget, a current phone or utilities bill, OK?"

"OK." I stare at her hard. "I got to go get all that *now?*"

"No, no relax, we're gonna give you a few tests; test your reading and math level, see whether to put you in pre-G.E.D. or G.E.D."

"What's the difference?"

"Well G.E.D. classes are for students whose basic skills are up to par and they're ready to just go into a class and start working on their G.E.D. Pre-G.E.D. is when the student needs some work to get to the level of the G.E.D. class."

"What level that?"

"Well, to enter G.E.D. classes a student should be able to read on an eighth-grade level. They should score 8.0 or better on the TABE reading test."

"I was in the ninfe grade at I.S. 146."

"Then," Cornrows smile at me, "you should have no problem."

"What's the problem?" I axes the fat dark-skin woman who is looking over my shoulder at my answer sheet. She got leggings like mine 'cept hers black. She got on blue blouse, look nice, like silk. She look OK I guess. I like light-skin people, they nice. I likes slim people too. Mama fat black, if I weigh two hundred she weigh three. The fat lady is looking at me. I looks back, she ain' answered my question.

"What's the problem?" I axes again.

"Well I think maybe you may need to take the test again—"

"You the teacher?"

"One of them."

"What you teach?"

"I teach the G.E.D. class."

"Who the other teacher?"

"Ms Rain."

"What she teach?"

"Ms Rain teaches the pre-G.E.D. reading class."

I know thas where I b'long, "Thas where I b'long," I tell her.

"Hmmm," go fat black heifer and look at me. I don't believe this bitch no teacher.

"Do you want to take the test again?"

"No."

For me this nuffin' new. There has always been something wrong wif the tesses. The tesses paint a picture of me wif no brain. The tesses paint a picture of me an' my muver—my whole family, we more than dumb, we invisible. One time I seen us on TV. It was a show of spooky shit, an' castles, you know shit be all haunted. And the peoples, well some of them was peoples and some of them was vampire peoples. But the real peoples did not know it till it was party time. You know crackers eating roast turkey and champagne and shit. So it's five of 'em sitting on the couch; and one of 'em git up and take a picture. Got it? When picture develop (it's insta-matic) only *one* person on the couch. The other peoples did not exist. They vampires. They eats, drinks, wear clothes, talks, fucks, and stuff but when you git right down to it they don't exist.

I big, I talk, I eats, I cooks, I laugh, watch TV, do what my muver say. But I can see when the picture come back I don't exist. Don't nobody want me. Don't nobody need me. I know who I am. I know who they say I am—vampire sucking the system's blood. Ugly black grease to be wipe away, punish, kilt, changed, finded a job for.

I wanna say I am somebody. I wanna say it on sub-way, TV, movie, LOUD. I see the pink faces in suits look over top of my head. I watch myself disappear in their eyes, their tesses. I talk loud but still I don't exist.

I see it over and over, the real people, the people who show up when the picture come back; and they are pritty people, girls with little titties like buttons and legs like long white straws. Do all white people look like pictures? No, 'cause the white people at school is fat and cruel like evil witches from fairy tales but they exist. Is it because they white? If Mrs Lichenstein who have elephant stomach and garbage smell from her pussy exist, why don't I? Why can't I see myself, *feel* where I end and begin. I sometimes look in the pink people in suits eyes, the men from bizness, and they

look way above me, put me out of their eyes. My fahver
don't see me really. If he did he would know I was like a
white girl, a *real* person, inside. He would not climb on
me from forever and stick his dick in me 'n get me
inside on fire, bleed, I bleed then he slap me. Can't he
see I am a girl for flowers and thin straw legs and a place
in the picture. I been out the picture so long I am used
to it. But that don't mean it don't hurt. Sometimes I
pass by store window and somebody fat dark skin, old
looking, someone look like my muver look back at me.
But I know it can't be my muver 'cause my muver is at
home. She have not left home since Little Mongo was
born. Who I see? I stand in tub sometime, look my
body, it stretch marks, ripples. I try to hide myself, then
I try to show myself. I ax my muver for money to git my
hair done, clothes. I know the money she got for me—
from my baby. She usta give me money; now every time
I ax for money she say I took her husband, her man.
Her man? Please! Thas my mutherfuckin' fahver! I
hear her tell someone on phone I am heifer, take her
husband, I'm fast. What it take for my muver to see me?
Sometimes I wish I was not alive. But I don't know how
to die. Ain' no plug to pull out. 'N no matter how bad I
feel my heart don't stop beating and my eyes open in
the morning. I hardly have not seen my daughter since
she was a little baby. I never stick my bresses in her
mouth. My muver say what for? It's outta style. She say
I never do you. What that child of yours need tittie for?
She retarded. Mongoloid. Down Sinder.

What tess say? I don't give a fuck. I look bitch teacher woman in face, trying to see do she see *me* or the tess. But I don't care now what anybody see. I see something, somebody. I got baby. So what. I feel proud 'cept it's baby by my fahver and that make me not in picture again.

"Again?"

Is she saying something? It's teacher woman, "Would you like to take the test again?"

I shake my head no. What for, it gonna be the same, I ain't change. I still me, Precious. She say I in first class which meet Monday, Wednesday, and Friday, 9 a.m. to 12 noon. I say, "I usta going to school everyday all day." She asks me if I could get use to something else. I don't say nuffin', then I say loud, "YES."

First thing I see when I wake up is picture of Farrakhan's face on the wall. I love him. He is against crack addicts and crackers. Crackers is the cause of everything bad. It why my father ack like he do. He has forgot he is the Original Man! So he fuck me, fuck me, beat me, have a chile by me. When he see I'm pregnant the first time he disappear. I think for years, for a long time I know that much.

After my baby and me come out of the hospital my muver take us down to welfare; say I is mother but just a chile and she taking care of bofe us'es. So really all she did was add my baby to her budget. She already on the 'fare wit' me so she just add my daughter. I could be on the 'fare for myself now, I think. I'm old enuff. I'm 16. But I'm not sure I know how to be on my own. I have to say sometimes I hate my muver. She don't love me. I wonder how she could love Little Mongo (thas my daughter). Mongo sound Spanish don't it? Yeah, thas why I chose it, but what it is is short for Mongoloid Down Sinder, which is what she is; sometimes what I feel I is. I feel so stupid sometimes. So ugly, worth nuffin'. I could just sit here wif my muver everyday wif the shades drawed, watching TV, eat, watch TV, eat. Carl come over fuck us'es. Go from room to room, slap me on my ass when he through, holler WHEEE WHEEE! Call me name Butter Ball Big Mama Two Ton of Fun. I hate hear him talk more than I hate fuck. Sometimes fuck feel good. That confuse me, everything get swimming for me, floating like for days sometimes. I just sit in back classroom, somebody say something I shout on 'em, hit 'em; rest of the time I mine my bizness. I was on my way to graduate from I.S. 146 'n then fuckface Miz Lichenstein mess shit up. I . . . , in my inside world, I am so pretty, like a advertisement girl on commercial, 'n someone ride up here in car, someone look like the son of that guy that got kilt when he was president a long time ago or Tom Cruise—or anybody like that pull up here in a car and I be riding like on TV chile—JeeZUS! It's 8 a.m. o'clock! I know I woketed up at 6 a.m., lord where the time go! I got to get dress for school. I got to be at school by 9 a.m. Today is first day. I been tessed. I been incomed eligible. I got Medicaid card and proof of address. All that shit. I is ready. Ready for school. School something (this *nuthin'*!). School gonna help me get out dis house. I gotta throw some water on my ass and git up. What I'm gonna wear what I'm gonna wear? One thing I do got is clothes, thanks to my muver's charge at Lane Bryant 'n man sell hot shit. Come to building go from door to door, I got your size he call out in hallway I got your size. I got to get dress. I wear my pink stretch pants? I think so, wif my black pesint blouse. I go splash some water on my ass, which mean I wash serious between my legs and underarm. I don't smell like my muver. I *don't*. I ain' got no money for lunch or McDonald's for breakfast. I take piece of ham out frigidare, wrap it in aluminum foil, I'll eat it walking down Lenox, not as good as Egg McMuffin but beat nuffin'. I double back to my room. On top my dresser is notebook. Ol' Cornrows say bring self, pencil, and notebook. I got self, pencil, and notebook. Can I get a witness! I'm outta here!

I always did like school, jus' seem school never did like me. Kinnergarden and first grade I don't talk, they laff at that. Second grade my cherry busted. I don't want to think that now. I look across the street at McDonald's but I ain't got no money so I unwrap ham and take a bite. I'm gonna ask Mama for some money when she get her check, plus the school gonna give me a stipend, thas money for goin' to school. Secon' grade they laffes at HOW I talk. So I stop talking. What for? Secon' thas when the "I'mma joke" start. When I go sit down boyz make fart sounds wif they mouf like it's me fartin'. When I git up they snort snort hog grunt sounds. So I jus' stop getting up. What for? Thas when I start to pee on myself. I just sit there, it's like I paralyze or some shit. I don't move. I *can't* move. Secon' grade teacher HATE me. Oh that woman hate me. I look at myself in the window of the fried chicken joint between 127th and 126th. I look good in my pink stretch pants. Woman at Lane Bryant on one-two-five say no reason big girls can't wear the latest, so I wear it. But boyz still laff me, what could I wear that boyz don't laff? Secon' grade is when I just start to sit there. All day. Other kids run all around. Me, Claireece P. Jones, come in 8:55 a.m., sit down, don't move till the bell ring to go home. I wet myself. Don't know why I don't get up, but I don't. I jus' sit there and pee. Teacher ack all care at first, then scream, then get Principal. Principal call Mama and who else I don't remember. Finally Principal say, Let it be. Be glad thas all the trouble she give you. Focus on the ones who *can* learn, Principal say to teacher. What that mean? Is she one of the ones who can't?

My head hurt. I gotta eat something. It's 8:45 a.m. I gotta be at school at 9 a.m. Ham gone. I ain't got no money. I turn back to chicken place. Walk in cool tell lady, Give me a basket. Chicken look like last night's but people in there buying it ol' or not. Lady ax, Fries? I say, Potato salad. Potato salad in the refrigerator in the back. I know that. Lady turn roun' to go in back, I grab chicken and roll, turn, run out, and cut down one-two-six stuffing chicken in my mouth. "Scarf Big Mama!" this from crack addict standing in front abandoned building. I don't even turn my head—crack addicts is *disgusting*! Give race a bad name, lost in the hells of norf america crack addicts is.

I look at watch, 8:57 a.m.! But shit I'm almost there! Coming around the corner of 126th onto Adam Clayton Powell Jr Blvd. I throws the chicken bones into the trash can on the corner, wipe the grease off my mouth with the

roll then stuff rest of roll in my mouf, run across 125th,
and I'm there! I'm in the elevator moving up when I realize I left my notebook and pencil in the chicken place!
Goddam! And it's 9:05 a.m. not 9:00 a.m. Oh well
teacher nigger too. Don't care if she teacher, don't no
niggers start on time. The elevator goes Bing! I step out.
My class last door on left. My teacher Miz Rain.

I'm walking across the lobby room real real slow. Full of
chicken, bread; usually that make me not want to cry
remember, but I feel like crying now. My head is like
the swimming pool at the Y on one-three-five. Summer
full of bodies splashing, most in shallow end; one, two
in deep end. Thas how all the time years is swimming
in my head. First grade boy say, Pick up your lips
Claireece 'fore you trip over them. Call me shoe shine
shinola. Second grade I is fat. Thas when fart sounds
and pig grunt sounds start. No boyfriend no girlfriends.
I stare at the blackboard pretending. I don't know what
I'm pretending—that trains ain' riding through my
head sometime and that yes, I'm reading along with the
class on page 55 of the reader. Early on I realize no one
hear the TV set voices growing out blackboard but me,
so I try not to answer them. Over in deepest end of the
pool (where you could drown if not for fine lifeguard
look like Bobby Brown) is me sitting in my chair at my
desk and the world turn to whirring sound, everything
is noise, teacher's voice white static. My pee pee open

hot stinky down my thighs sssssss splatter splatter. I wanna die I hate myself HATE myself. Giggles giggles but I don't move I barely breathe I just sit. They giggle. I stare straight ahead. They talk me. I don't say nuffin'.

Seven, he on me almost every night. First it's just in my mouth. Then it's more more. He is intercoursing me. Say I can take it. Look you don't even bleed, virgin girls bleed. You not virgin. I'm *seven*.

I don't realize I've gone from walking real real slow to standing perfectly still. I'm in the lobby of first day of school Higher Education Alternative/Each One Teach One just standing there. I realize this 'cause Miz Rain done peeked her head out last door on the left and said, "You alright?" I know who she is 'cause Miss Cornrow with the glasses had done pointed her out to me after I finish testing and show me my teacher and classroom.

I make my feet move. I don't say anything. Nothing in my mouth to say. I move my feet some more. Miz Rain ask me if I'm in the A.B.E. class. I say yes. She say this is it and go back inside door. The first thing I see when I step through door is the windows, where we is is high up, no other buildings in the way. Sky blue blue. I looks around the room now. Walls painted lite ugly green. Miz Rain at her desk, her back to me, her face to the class and the windows. "Class" only about five, six other people. Miz Teacher turn around say, Have a seat. I stays standing at door. I swallow hard, start to, I think I'm gonna cry. I look Miz Teacher's long dreadlocky hair, look kinda nice but look kinda nasty too. My knees is shaking, I'm scared I'm gonna pee on myself, even though I has not done no shit like that in years. I don't know how I'm gonna do it, but I am—I look at the six chairs line up neat in the back of the room. I gotta get there.

The whole class quiet. Everybody staring at me. God don't let me cry. I takes in air through my nose, a big big breath, then I start to walk slow to the back. But something like birds or light fly through my heart. An' my feet stop. At the first row. An' for the first time in my life I sits down in the front row (which is good 'cause I never could see the board from the back).

I ain' got no notebook, no money. My head is big 'lympic size pool, all the years, all the me's floating around glued shamed to desks while pee puddles get big near their feet. Man don't nobody know it but it ain' no joke for me to be here in this school. I glance above teacher's head at the wall. Is a picture of small dark lady with face like prune and dress from the oldern days. I wonder who she is. Teacher sit at desk marking roll sheet, got on purple dress and running shoes. She dark, got nice face, big eyes, and hair like I already said. My muver do not like niggers wear they hair like that! My muver say Farrakhan OK but he done gone too far. Too far where I wanna ax. I don't know how *I* feel about people with hair like that.

The teacher is talking.

"You'll need a notebook like this," she hold up a black 'n white 79-cent notebook just like what I left in chicken place. As she talking girl walk in.

"It's nine thirty-seven," teacher say. "Jo Ann you *late*."

"I had to stop and get something to eat."

"Next time stay where you stop. Starting tomorrow this door will be locked at nine o'clock!"

"I better be on the side that's in," grumble Jo Ann.

"We agree on that," say teacher, she look Jo Ann in eye. She not scared of Jo Ann. Well gone Miz Rain.

"We got some new people—"

"I found something!" Jo Ann shout.

"I beg your pardon," say teacher but you can see she ain' beggin' nothin', she mad.

"No, I'm sorry Ms Rain"—I see right now Jo Ann is clown—"but I jus' want to say, do anyone need an extra notebook I foun' in the chicken place?"

"It's mine!" I say.

"Git a grip," Jo Ann say.

"I got one." I shocks myself saying that. "I left that book at Arkansas Jr. Fried Chicken on Lenox between one-two-seven and one-two-six this morning."

"Well I'll be a turkey's asshole!" Jo Ann screamed. "Thas where I found it."

I reaches my hand she smile me. Han' me my book, look at my stomach, say, "When you due?"

I say, "Not sure."

She frown, don't say nothing, and go sit a couple seats away from me in the row right behind me.

Miz Rain look pretty bent out of shape then melt, say, "We got more new people than old people today, so let's just go back to day one and git to know each other and figure out what we gonna do here together." I look at her weird. Ain' she spozed to *know* what we gonna do. How we gonna figure anything out. Weze ignerent. We here to learn, leas' I am. God I hope this don't be another . . . another . . . I don't know—another like before, yeah another like the years before.

"Let's try a circle," teacher say. Damn I just did sit myself down in front row and now we getting in a circle.

"We don't need all those chairs," teacher say waving at Jo Ann who dragging chairs from second row. "Just pull out five or six, however many of us it is, and put 'em in a little circle and then we'll put 'em back in rows after we finish introducing ourselves." She sit herself in one of the chairs and we all do the same (I mean she the teacher 'n all).

"OK," she say, "let's get to know each other a little bit uummm, let's see, how about your name, where you were born, your favorite color, and something you do good and why you're here."

"Huh?" Big red girl snort. Miss Rain go to board and say, "Number one, your name," then she write it, "number two, where you were born," and so on until it all on board:

1. name
2. where you were born
3. favorite color
4. something you do good
5. why you are here today

She sit back down say, "OK, I'll start. My name is Blue Rain—"

"Thas your real name!" This from girl with boy suit on.

"Um hmmm, that's my for real hope to die if I'm lying name."

"Your first name *Blue*?" same girl say.

"Um hmm," Ms Rain say this like she tired of mannish girl.

"Splain that!"

"Well," say Ms Rain real proper. "I don't feel I have to explain my name." She look at girl, girl git message. "Now as I was saying my name is Blue Rain. I was born in California. My favorite color is purple. What do I do good? Ummm, I sing purty good. And I'm here because my girlfriend used to teach here and she was out one day and asked me to substitute for her, then when she quit, they asked me did I want the job. I said yeah and I been here ever since."

I look around the circle, it's six people, not counting me. A big redbone girl, loud bug-out girl who find my notebook at chicken place, Spanish girl with light skin, then this brown-skin Spanish girl, and a girl my color in boy suit, look like some kinda butch.

Big Red talking now, "My name Rhonda Patrice Johnson." Rhonda big, taller than me, light skin but it don't do nuffin' for her. She ugly, got big lips, pig nose, she fat fat and her hair rusty color but short short.

"I was born in Kingston, Jamaica." Ain' that something! She don't talk funny at all like how coconut head peoples do. "My favorite color is blue, I cook good."

"What?" somebody say.

"Name it!" Rhonda shoot back.

"Peas 'n rice!"

"Yeah yeah," like why even mention somethin' so basic.

"Curry goat!"

"Yeah, you name it," Rhonda say. "My mother usta have a restaurant on Seventh Ave before she got sick, she taught me everything. I'm here," she say serious, "to bring my reading up so I could get my G.E.D."

The skinny light-skin Spanish girl speak, "My name is Rita Romero. I was born right here in Harlem. I'm here because I was an addict and dropped out of school and never got my reading and writing together. My favorite color is black." She smile messed up teef. "I guess you could tell that." We could looking at her clothes 'n shoes, all black.

"What you do good?" Rhonda ax.

"Hmm," she say, then in shaky voice real slow, "I'm a good mother, a very good mother."

Brown girl talk. We about the same color but I think thas all we got the same. I is *all* girl. Don't know here.

"My name is Jermaine."

Uh oh! Some kinda freak.

"My favorite color—"

"Tell us where you born first," Rhonda again.

Jermaine give Rhonda a piss on you look. Rhonda

cut her eyes at Jermaine like jump bad if you want to. Jermaine say she was born in the Bronx, still live there. Red her favorite color. She a good dancer. She come here 'cause she want to get away from negative influence of the Bronx.

Spanish girl Rita say, "You come to *Harlem* to get away from bad influence?"

Jermaine, which I don't have to tell you is a *boy's* name, say, "It's *who* you know and I know too many people in the Bronx baby."

"How did you find out about the program?" Miz Rain ax.

"A friend."

Miz Rain don't say nothin' else.

Girl foun' my notebook next. "Jo Ann is my name, rap is my game. My color is beige. My ambition is to have my own record layer."

Miz Rain look at her. I wonder myself what is a record layer.

"Where was you born and why you at this school," Rhonda ax. OK, I see Rhonda like to run things.

"I was born in King's County Hospital. My mother moved us to Harlem when I was nine years old. I'm here to get my G.E.D., then, well I'm already into the music industry. I just need to take care of the education thing so I can move on up."

Next girl speaks. "My name is Consuelo Montene-gro." Ooohhh she pretty Spanish girl, coffee-cream color wit long ol' good hair. Red blouse. "Why I'm here, favorite color—what's-alla dat shit?" She look Ms Rain in face, mad.

Miz Rain calm. Rain, nice name for her. Ack like she don't mind cursing, say, "It's just a way of breaking the ice, a way of getting to know each other better, by asking nonthreatening questions that allow you to share yourself with a group without having to reveal more of yourself than might be comfortable." She pause. "You don't have to do it if you don't want to."

"I don't want to," beautiful girl say.

Everybody looking at me now. In circle I see everybody, everybody see me. I wish for back of the class again for a second, then I think never that again, I kill myself first 'fore I let that happen.

"My name Precious Jones. I was born in Harlem. My baby gonna be borned in Harlem. I like what color— yellow, thas fresh. 'N I had a problem at my ol' school so I come here."

"Something you do good," Rhonda say.

"Nuffin'," I say.

"Everybody do something good," Ms Rain say in soft voice.

I shake my head, can't think of nuffin'. I'm staring at my shoes.

"One thing," Ms Rain.

"I can cook," I say. I keep my eyes on shoes. I never talk in class before 'cept to cuss teacher or kids if they fuck wif me.

Miz Rain talking about the class. "Periodically we'll be getting into a circle to talk and work but let's put our chairs back in rows for now and move on with our business. Well, first thing, this is a basic reading and writing class, a pre-G.E.D. adult literacy class, a class for beginning readers and writers. This is *not* a G.E.D. class—"

"This not G.E.D.?" Jermaine ax.

"No, it's not. This class is set up to teach students how to read and write," Miz Rain say.

"Shit I know how to read and write, I want to get my G.E.D.," Jo Ann say.

Miz Rain look tired, "Well then this class isn't for you. And I'd appreciate it if you watch your language, this *is* a school."

"Ain' shit to me—"

"Well then go, Jo Ann, why don't you just tip," Miz Rain seem like, you know, well *leave* bitch.

Spanish girl, Rita, say, "Well this here *is* for me. I can't read or write."

Rhonda come in, "I can a little, but I need help."

Jermaine look unsure.

Miz Rain, "If you think you want to be in the G.E.D. class all you have to do is come back to this room at one p.m. for placement testing." Jermaine don't move. Consuelo look to Jermaine but don't say nuffin'. Jo Ann say she be back at one, fuck this shit! She ain' illiterit. Miz Rain look at me. I'm the only one haven't spoken. I wanna say something but don't know how. I'm not use to talkin', how can I say it? I look Miz Rain. She say, "Well Precious, how about you, do you feel you're in the right place?"

I want to tell her what I always wanted to tell someone, that the pages, 'cept for the ones with pictures, look all the same to me; the back row I'm not in today; how I sit in a chair seven years old all day wifout moving. But I'm not seven years old. But I am crying. I look Miz Rain in the face, tears is coming down my eyes, but I'm not sad or embarrass.

"Is I Miz Rain," I axes, "is I in the right place?"

She hand me a tissue, say, "Yes, Precious, yes."

Miz Rain say class need a break. "BE BACK IN 15 MIN-UTES," she say real loud like a machine talk. I get up with the rest, goes out in the lobby. It's empty 'ceptin' us. The other classes don't be here till 12, Miz Rain say. Rhonda say she goin' to the store, anybody want somethin'? I want somethin' but I ain' got no money. Rita give her 50 cents say get chips, salt 'n vinegar, no salt 'n vinegar get plain. Rhonda look me, say, I got you. I look up in her eye. She smile. I feel like I'm gonna cry again. Everybody gonna think I'm a punk, crying, crying. I'm not used to this. But this what I always want, some friendly niceness. I say I pay you back. She say I know you will, what you want. I say barbecue potato chips. She gone! Rhonda move fast for a big girl.

Consuelo, the beautiful Spanish girl, sigh. "Ain' no

guys in our class." This like you know she los' her welfare check after it jus' been cash or somethin'.

Jermaine say, "Good."

Uh oh! Freaky deaky here. I move a little way from her. I don't want no one getting the wrong idea about *me*.

Back in class Miz Rain is telling us what we gonna do everyday. So she *do* know what's what. I was scared for a minute it be like before. Like before I got A in English and never say nuffin', do nuffin'. I sit in seat. I sit in seat everyday for 55 minutes, chair so far back it touch wall. After first day I don't see hear. I play TV in my mind— switch back 'n forth from TV to music videos where I'm dancing in little clothes, shit, *I'm* little.

"Every day," Miz Rain say, "we gonna read and write in our notebooks."

How we gonna write if we can't read? Shit, how we gonna write if we can't write! I don't remember never doing no writing before. My head spinning I'm scared maybe we, maybe this ain' class for me.

Miz Rain talkin'. She say, Chinese saying, I knew she was crazy—we ain' CHINESE! She real serious now, say, "The longest journey begin with a single step." What the fuck that spozed to mean. This school not *Star Trek*. Rita, Spanish girl, looking at Miz Rain like she done see god. Rhonda sitting straight up in her seat. Jermaine looking out the side of her eyes at Consuelo. Consuelo looking at her nails.

Miz Rain hold up notebook, say, "You going to need

one notebook like this"—like what I awready got—
"and another notebook—loose-leaf or spiral, to keep
your notes and class work in." Complicated complicated, Chinese journeys, 2 books, write 'n you don't
know how—

Jermaine say, "Where we gonna begin?"

Miz Rain say, "At the beginning," and pick a piece of
chalk out her purse and walk to the board. She write *A*
on the board, she hand the chalk to Jermaine. Jermaine
write *B*. Jermaine hand it to Consuelo, she write *C*.
Consuelo hand it to Rhonda she write *D*. Rhonda hand
it to Rita. Rita take a step and start to cry. Miz Rain say
we all in this together. All us say *E* real loud, Rita go up
'n write *E*, hand me chalk 'n I write *F* and so it go. Then
we sits back down all at once, that make us laff, and Miz
Rain say this is the beginning, there are twenty-six letters in the alphabet, they all have a sound. These letters
make up all the words in our language. Please open
your notebook, write the date, October 19, 1987, then
write the alphabet in your notebook.

After we write the alphabet in our notebook we
recite it out loud together. Miz Rain say go home and
practice saying it 'n saying it. On Wednesday she gonna
ask each one to stand up and deliver. Jermaine say,
"Spoze I know it already?" Miz Rain say, "Then it
should be no problem for you." But I remember Jermaine write *Q* after *O* instead of *P*. I remember that. I
gonna practice. I sure am. Miz Rain say on Wednesday
she gonna talk to us about keeping a journal. Tell us

again we gotta bring in another notebook for to be our journal. How is a journal different from a notebook I wanna ask but I never asked a question before in school.

I feels little music in my head. I know I'm tripping. I feel the baby in my stomach. Don't feel good. I try not to think about my stomach big like this—the heavy pressing down on my bladder parts, like a fucking water-melon under my skin. See a doctor? My muver want me to go get on welfare. But I'm on welfare—hers. It's like you know, I know she ain't gonna get money for me I ain' in school; she gonna always get money for my daughter 'cause she retarded. Maybe somethin' gonna be wrong wif this baby too. I don't care, maybe if new baby Down Sinder I can get my own check.

But I don't know if I want check. I wonder what reading books be like.

Miz Rain say we almost finished for the day, say she wanna spend some time with each student in little office room to side before we go. Say she gonna call us out one by one in alphabetical order. I feel panicking panicking— I don't know alphabetical order—whas that!

Miz Rain say she be in little office, get up, then say unsure like, I never seen teacher unsure ('less you gettin' ready to hit 'em). She say, "Yall can call me Blue if you want." I look her like she crazy—why we want that? I might say some bad things I get mad or somebody fuck with me or somethin', but I try to show *respect* for peoples. So I say to myself, No, Miz Rain, I don't want call you Blue. "Or . . . or," she says, "Rain, some people jus' call me Rain." Her voice got a country soun' to it. Jermaine says, "I like that, Rain." Don' nobody else say nothing.

Rhonda git up after Miz Rain gone. Rhonda something.

"OK, look at alphabets," she say loud. I wanna say you ain' got to talk so loud, but I don't. "OK," she say, "which name go first."

Consuelo say, "I guess that's me." I wanna know why but I don't ask. I see Rhonda somethin' else of a lady. Wifout me axin', she say, "You git it Precious?" I says, "No." She say, "Look at the alphabets—anybody name start wif *A* in here." I shake my head. "*B*?" I shake my head no. "*C*?" Don't shake my head. "Good!" she say. She say, "Consuelo start wif *C*, she first." She write:

1. Consuelo

Who next? she axes me. I don't know. She point to *D, E, F, G*. I look Jermaine. Jermaine say, "My name start wif *J*." Rhonda go, *H, I, J*—

I point Jermaine. Now it's:

1. Consuelo
2. Jermaine

Miz Rain stick head in door. Rhonda say, "Give us five." Miz Rain smile us 'n go back out. Rhonda go, "*K, L, M, N, O, P*—"

"*P* for Precious!" I hollers. "I'm next."

"You got it, you got it," Rhonda say.

1. Consuelo
2. Jermaine
3. Precious

"*Q, R*—"

"Rita!" Thas Rita shout that. "I'm *R* too." Rhonda quiz us, "Which go first me or her?" Jermaine say, "You do," to Rhonda. I don't know why. I remember Jo Ann. I know that *J* like Jermaine. If she wasn't gone where would she go, in front Jermaine? Behind?

Miz Rain come to the door say, first person. Consuelo go. Then Miz Rain come back say, Next, Jermaine go. Then she call me. We go in little room off side. "This gonna be painless," Miz Rain say, "I just want you to read a page from this little book." All the air go out my body. I grab my stomach. Miz Rain look scared. "Precious!" My head water. I see bad things. I see my daddy. I see TVs I hear rap music I want something to eat I want fuck feeling from Daddy I want die I want die.

"Precious! Are you alright! Breathe! Relax and breathe. Should I call an ambulance? Nine-one-one? Your mother—"

"NO!"

"What's wrong Precious?"

I struggles for air, "I . . . the pages look alike to me." I breave in deep, there I said it.

Miz Rain sigh sad like. "I think I understand you, Precious. But for now, I want you to try, push yourself Precious, go for it."

I reach out my hand for book.

"Just do the best you can, if you don't know a word skip—" She stop. "Just look at the page and say the words you do know."

I look at the page, it's some people at the beach. Some is white, some is orange and gray (I guess thas spozed to be colored).

"What do you think the story is about Precious?"

"Peoples at the beach."

"That's right." Miz Rain point to a letter, ask me what is it. I say, "*A*." She point to some more letters. I don't say nuffin'. "Do you know that word?" No, I don't. "Do you know the letters?" Umm hmmm. She point *D*, then *A*, then *Y*. She say do you know that word? No I don't but I say silence. She say, " 'Day,' that word is 'day.' " She point back at *A*, then "DAY," then point at *A*, *T*, say, "What's that word?" I say, "Ate." She say, "Good! Almost! That word is 'at.' " Then point next word. I say, "The"; then she point last word. I say, "Beach," but I'm not sure, I know *B* in "beach," no *B* in that word. She say, " 'Shore,' that word is 'shore,' that's almost like 'beach,' very good very good," she say. Then she say in soft voice like cat purr (I always wishted I had a cat), "Can you read the whole thing?" I say, "A Day at the Beach." She says very good and closes the book. I want to cry. I want to laugh. I want to hug kiss Miz Rain. She make me feel good. I never readed nuffin' before.

Wednesday can't come fast enuff I'm thinking as I walk down one-two-five. I loves Harlem, especially 125th Street. Lotta stuff out here. You could see we got culchure. I gotta ask my muver for some money for journal book and pay Rhonda back for chips. This gonna be good school for me I know it.

My muver is in the middle of her stories when I come in—TV, TV. She shout on me the minute I open the door.

"Bring your fat ass in here!"

What she think I was doing? I'm tired; I don't want no trouble.

"Where you sneak your ass off to this morning?"

She look like whale on couch. My muver have not left the house in, let's see—1983, '84, '85, '86, 'n now '87. Ever since Little Mongo was born. Social worker come here. I be at school. My grandmuver, Toosie, bring Little Mongo over on days social worker come; game is Little Mongo live here, my mama take care of Little Mongo and me. My mama get check 'n food stamps for me 'n Lil Mongo. But it's *my* baby. Little Mongo is money for me!

"You hear me talking to you! I said where you sneak your ass off to this morning!"

"School!" I shout back. "I was school!"

"You was school?" Mama mimic me how I talk. I hate that! She know what I mean. "You lying whore!"

"Not!"

"You is! The welfare done called here, saying they is removing you from my budget 'cause you not in regular attendance at school."

JeeZUS! Where she been! I told her I got kickted out. I been home three weeks, twenty-four seven. She here when Mrs Lichenstein's white ass come here. I mean Mama what's the deal! Who stupid, me or Mama?

"What you staring at?"

To get to my room I got to walk past Mama. I jus' wanna go to my room.

"I ain' had no breakfast," Mama say.

Oh, so that's it. She want me to cook. Mad 'cause I ain' cook 'fore I left. Shit, get tired of cooking for her. It hard for Mama to stand up long. I look at her. She ain' circus size yet but she getting there. Usta be when I go to regular school Mama make me fix breakfast, bring it to her room 'fore I leave. But since I be outta school I just fix it a little later. She know today I was goin' to alternative.

"I tole you I was goin' to school today."

"Forget school! You better git your ass on down to welfare!"

"I gonna get stipend for school."

"Fool fuck a stipend! What's that. I said take your ass down to welfare NOW!"

"Now?" She know I got to be there at 7 a.m. if I

gonna get to talk to anybody. Welfare very crowded nowadays. "I go in the morning first thing."

Same thing in me when I try to hit Mrs Lichenstein 'n when I grabbed the knife in the dishwater—only deeper. I think my mind a TV set smell like between my muver's legs. I stupid. I ain' got no education even tho' I not miss days of school. I talks funny. The air floats like water wif pictures around me sometime. Sometimes I can't breathe. I'm a good girl. I don't fucks boyz but I'm pregnant. My fahver fuck me. And she know it. She kick me in my head when I'm pregnant. She take *my* money. Money for Little Mongo should be mine. A Day at the Beach Shore A Day A Day ABC Alphabetical order CD ABCD. I grab my notebook. I look at my muver.

"I go to welfare tomorrow—Tuesday. Wednesday I go to school. Monday, Wednesday, and Friday I go to school."

I look Mama. This baby feel like a watermelon between my bones getting bigger and my ankles feelin' tight 'cause they swoled. I sigh. This gonna end, even if it end by me stop breathing. Thas what I want sometimes. Sometime I hurt so bad I want to not wake up, want breathing to stop in my sleep. Have me *don't* wake up. Other times I start to go a huh a huh ahuh ahuh A HUH A HUH and I grab my chess 'cause I can't breathe, then I *WANT* breathin' bad.

I try to forget I got baby in me. I hated borning the first one. No fun. Hurt. Now again. I think my daddy. He stink, the white shit drip off his dick. Lick it lick it. I

HATE that. But then I feel the hot sauce hot cha cha feeling when he be fucking me. I get so confuse. I HATE him. But my pussy be popping. He say that, "Big Mama your pussy is popping!" I HATE myself when I feel good.

"How long you gonna stand there like you retarded."

I start to tell her don't, don't call me that, but all, everything, is out me. I jus' want to lay down, listen to radio, look at picture of Farrakhan, a *real* man, who don't fuck his daughter, fuck children. Everything feel like it is too big for my mind. Can't nuffin' fit when I think 'bout Daddy.

"I'm tired." Why I say that, she don't care.

"Fix us some lunch, it's way pas' lunch. You done ate?"

"I had some potato chips."

"Thas all?"

I remember ham 'n chicken, don't say nuffin', ax her, "What you want?"

"I don't know, see what's in there. If not nuffin' in there, get stamps out my purse and go to store 'n get us'es somethin' to eat."

ABCDEFGHIJKLMNOPABCDEFGHIJKLMNO PQRS. There are 26 letters in our alphabet. Each letter has a sound. A Day at the Beach Shore ABCDEFGHI JKLMNOPQRSTUVWXYZ.

That night I dream I am not in me but am awake listening to myself choking, going a huh a huh A HUH A HUH A HUH. I am walking around trying to find where I am, where the sound is coming from. I know I will choke to death I don't find myself. I walk to my muver's room but it look different, she look different. I look like little baby almost. She is talkin' sweet to me like sometimes Daddy talks. I am choking between her legs A HUH A HUH. She is smelling big woman smell. She say suck it, lick me Precious. Her hand is like a mountain pushing my head down. I squeeze my eyes shut but choking don't stop, it get worse. Then I open my eyes and look. I look at little Precious and big Mama and feel hit feeling, feel like killing Mama. But I don't, instead I call little Precious and say, Come to Mama but I means me. Come to *me* little Precious. Little Precious look at me, smile, and start to sing: ABCDEFG . . .

Wednesday morning Jo Ann back. She not like G.E.D. I guess. Say she need a little brush up before she go to G.E.D. Miz Rain don't say nuffin' till she hear the brush up stuff, then Miz Rain say, "Are you in the right class Jo Ann? This is a class to learn reading and writing, this is not a brush up for G.E.D." Jo Ann look hate at Miz Rain. I like Miz Rain. I see what she doing, I think. Jo Ann tryin' to act like she ain' one of us. Miz Rain tryin' to git her to 'cept herself for where she at. She ain' no G.E.D. girl, leas' not yet.

Miz Rain call roll: Jermaine Hicks, Rhonda Johnson, Precious Jones, Consuelo Montenegro, Jo Ann Rogers, Rita Romero. Everybody here. Miz Rain ax, "Who wishes to start?" Jo Ann and Jermaine look at her like what she talking. I go to stand up, see Rita Romero done beat me to my feet. She slim, not pretty but she got that light skin that stand for something. Miz Rain look me, say, Gone git up Precious, you can recite together. Rita smile half a smile at me; it's real, but only half 'cause she don't want to show rot teef. I look in her eye, she nod, we go together: ABCDEFGHI JKLMNOPQRSTUVWXYZ.

Then everybody go except Jo Ann. Then Miz Rain ax us to get out our journal books. Mama don't give me no money but I took the change from the food stamps when I was shopping to git one. I got Rhonda's 50 cents too from bottles and cans.

"This is your journal," Miz Rain say. "You're going to write in it everyday." Jo Ann look disgusted, like yeah *right*! One minute we doin' ABCs, next minute we spozed to be writing. Miz Rain give her look like fuck you bitch. I can tell Miz Rain don't like her but she don't say nothin'. She jus' tell us we gonna write in our journals for fifteen minutes everyday.

How, I wonder.

"How," Rhonda say out loud, "*how* we gonna write for fifteen minutes if we can't spell?"

What we gonna write if we could spell, I wonder.

"What," Jermaine throw her two cents in, "what we gonna write?"

Miz Rain say, "Write what's on your mind, push yourself to see the letters that represent the words you're thinking." She turn to me ax real fast, "Precious what's on your mind?" I say, "What?'" She say, "What you was thinking just then." I go to open my mouf. She say, "Don't say it, *write* it." I say, "I can't." She say, "Don't say that." She say, "DO what I say, write what you was thinking."

I do:

li Mg o mi m

She tell everyone to not talk and to write for the next fifteen minutes. Everybody is trying something. After time up Miz Rain come to my book ax me to read what I wrote. I reads: "Little Mongo on my mind."

Underneaf what I wrote Miz Rain write what I said in pencil.

li Mg o mi m
(Little Mongo on my mind)

Then she write:

Who is Little Mongo?

She read me what she wrote, tell me to *write* my answer to her question in the book. I copy Little Mongo's name from where Miz Rain had wrote it.

PUSH

Litte mony is mi cie

Miz Rain read, "Little Mongo is my child?" She have question in her voice. I say, "Yes yes." Miz Rain know Little Mongo is my child 'cause I wrote it in my journal. I am happy to be writing. I am happy to be in school. Miz Rain say we gonna write everyday, that mean home too. 'N she gonna write back everyday. Thas great.

I go home. I'm so lonely there. I never notice before. I'm so busy getting beat, cooking, cleaning, pussy and asshole either hurting or popping. School I a joke: black monster, Big Bertha, Blimp B54 where are you? 'N the TV's in my head always static on, flipping picture. So much pain, shame—I never feel the loneliness. It such a small thing compare to your daddy climb on you, your muver kick you, slave you, feel you up. But now since I been going to school I feel lonely. Now since I sit in circle I realize all my life, all my life I been outside of circle. Mama give me orders, Daddy porno talk me, school never did learn me.

It been a month now. I runs in from school nowadays. I don't pretend I'm not pregnant no more. I let it above my neck, in my head. Not that I didn't know it before but now it's like part of me; more than something stuck in me, growing in me, making me bigger. I run past my muver into my room. I wish I had TV in my room. My muver never let me have TV. She say come sit with her. I don't wanna.

I sit in my room. I know too who I'm pregnant for. But I can't change that. Abortion is a sin. I hate bitches who kill they babies. They should kill *them*, see how they like it! I talk to baby. Boy be nice. Girl might be retarded, like me? But I not retarded.

I bet chu one thing, I bet chu my baby can read. Bet a mutherfucker that! Betcha he ain' gonna have no dumb muver.

I look down my stomach. I'm some big now. I'm only seven months but I know I look nine. I mean I am *big*. Scale just stop at 200 but I know if it a different scale like hospital scale it just keep going. I'm going to doctor tomorrow. Miz Rain fall *out*, I mean she fall out! when she finded out I ain' been to doctor. *PRENATAL! PRENATAL!* The whole damn class is screamin' *preeeenatal!* Whas that! You gotta this, they say, and you gotta that— I don't gotta though. I don't tell them I had first baby on kitchen floor. Muver kicking me, pains whipping me. Who gonna believe some shit like that?

I look Farrakhan. I look out window at dirt bricks of other building, no sky like school. I got 'nother poster on wall now. Miz Rain give me poster like what we got on wall at school. Thas Harriet nex' to Farrakhan. She leaded over 300 black people out of slavery. You seen *Roots*? I ain't. Miz Rain say see *Roots*, find out what it's all about.

I put my han' on my stomach. I sit here, res' awhile

'fore Mama call me to fix dinner or clean up. It's 26 letters in the alphabet. Each letter got sound. Put sound to letters, mix letters together and get words. You got words. "Baby," start wif *B*, *b* for "baby," I says in nice soft voice. Soon as he git born I'ma start doing the ABCs. This my baby. My muver took Little Mongo but she ain' taking this one. I am comp'tant. I was comp'-tant enough for her husband to fuck. She ain' come in here and say, Carl Kenwood Jones—thas wrong! Git off Precious like that! Can't you see Precious is a beautiful chile like white chile in magazines or on toilet paper wrappers. Precious is a blue-eye skinny chile whose hair is long braids, long long braids. Git off Precious, fool! It time for Precious to go to the gym like Janet Jackson. It time for Precious hair to be braided. Get off my chile nigger!

No, she never say that. Miz Rain say value. Values determine how we live much as money do. I say Miz Rain stupid there. All I can think she don't know to have NOTHIN'. Never breathe and wait for check, check; cry when check late. Check important. Most important. My mama not getting no check for me, I think she be done killed me a long time ago (well maybe not kill me, but thas how I *feel*). Miz Rain say feelin's is important. White woman on the news leave her daddy in desert in a wheelchair when checks run out. He had Alhammer disease. Bitch leave him under a cactus tree wif teddy bear. Don't tell me 'bout check not important.

Mama say this new school ain' shit. Say you can't learn nuffin' writing in no book. Gotta git on that computer you want some money. When they gonna teach you how to do the computer. But Mama wrong. I is learning. I'm gonna start going to Family Literacy class on Tuesdays. Important to read to baby after it's born. Important to have colors hanging from the wall. Listen baby, I puts my hand on my stomach, breathe deep. Listen baby (I writes in my notebook):

A is fr Afrc
  (*for Africa*)
B is for u bae
  (*you baby*)
C is cl w bk
  (*colored we black*)
D is dog
E is el l/m
  (*evil like mama*)
F is Fuck
G is Jerm bt Jer j
  (*Jermaine but Jermaine J*)
ok G is gunn
H hm
  (*home*)
I I somb
  (*somebody*)
J Jer
  (*Jermaine*)
k kl
  (*kill*)

PUSH

l lv
(*love*)

M frknka rl m
(*Farrakhan real man*)

N nf kkk
(*North America   America=KKK*)

O op
(*open*)

P ph
(*punks*)

Q qee litee
(*Queen Latifah*)

R srt
(*respect*)

S stp
(*stop*)

T 2 tn
(*two ton*)

V vt
(*vote*)

W wll
(*well*)

X ma m ml
(*main man Malcolm*)

Z zk
(*zonked, mean like high*)

Listen baby, Muver love you. Muver not dumb. Listen baby: ABCDEFGHIJKLMNOPQRSTUVW XYZ.

Thas the alphabet. Twenty-six letters in all. Them letters make up words. Them words everything.

III

Boy. It's a boy. Borned at Harlem Hospital January 15, 1988. Abdul Jamal Louis Jones. That is my baby's name. Abdul mean servant of god; Jamal, I forgot; Louis for Farrakhan, of course. At school, new girl Joyce, bring me a book wif African names. I awready had known, Abdul, if it a boy. But I didn't know what it mean.

My name mean somethin' valuable—Precious. Claireece, that somebody else's name. I don't know where my muver get that shit from.

Well, I don't know 'bout baby, I'm happy 'bout baby, I'm sad about baby. Social worker come. I talk to her. She ask 'bout Little Mongo. I tell her Little Mongo wif my grandmother over on St Nicholas Ave. I probably shouldn't have done that. But I was tired. Tired of game, lying. Miz Rain said she read the truth shall set you free; say she not sure she believe it herself. Well, this truth gonna cause Mama to get kicked off welfare. 'Cause what she had been telling the 'fare is Mongo was living with her and she was taking care of bofe of us, so she was getting check for two dependent peoples and stuff. I don't know what's going to happen next. I know I gonna get my own money, but what that if I still in my mama's house? I need my own place, welfare don't give you that much. But main thing above everything else I want to go back to school. Thas all I think about—what they doing? What they reading? Did I miss the feel trip? I think I did.

November was my birthday, I don't tell nobody so don't nobody know. But I light a candle for myself. I glad Precious Jones was born. I like baby I born. It gets to suckes from my bress. First I don't like that. It hurt feel sore, then I like it. He's a good baby. But he's not mine. I mean, he is mine, I push him out my pussy, but I didn't meet a boy 'n fall in love, sex up 'n have a baby.

I think I was rape.

I think what my fahver do is what Farrakhan said the white man did to the black woman. Oh it was terrible and he dood it in front of the black man; that's really terrible. Yeah, on the video, Farrakhan say during slavery times the white man just walk out to the slavery Harlem part where the niggers live separate from the mansions where the white people live and he take any black woman he want and if he feel like it he jus' gone and do the do on top of her even if her man there. This spozed to hurt the black man even more than it hurt the woman getting rape—for the black man to have to see this raping.

My baby is pretty baby. I don't not love him. He is a rapist's baby. But that's OK, Miz Rain say we is a nation of raped children, that the black man in America today is the product of rape.

Still I don't want nobody to know but I tell again like when I was twelve. How can I say baby's fahver unknown when I know?

School, of everything, I know I want to get back to school. I got little baby suckes at my tittie, at my bress. I love Abdul. He normal. But I ain'? I want to go back to school. Abdul in my way. Abdul can not go to Higher Education/Each One Teach One. What I'm gonna do? I love my baby but he ain' mine, he is but I didn't fuck for him. I was raped by my fahver. Now instead of life for me I got Abdul. But I love Abdul. I want go school love abdul schoolabdulschoolabdul.

I write Miz Rain in my journal, when she come hospital she write me back like school:

Dr Miz Ms Rain,
all yr I sit cls I nevr lrn
(*all years I sit in class I never learn*)
bt I gt babe agn Babe bi my favr
(*but I got baby again Babe by my father*)
I wis i had boy____ but I don
(*I wish I had a boyfriend but I don't*)
ws i had su me fucks a boy lke
(*wish I had excuse me, fucks a boy like*)
or girl den i fel rite dat I have to qk skool
(*other girls then I feel right that I have to quit school*)
i lv baby abcdefghijklmnopqrstuvwxyz
(*I love baby*)

PUSH

Dear Precious,

   Don't forget to put the date, 1/18/88, on your journal entries.

   I am glad you love your baby. I think a beautiful young girl like you should get a chance to get an education. I think your first responsibility has to be to yourself. You should not drop out of school. COME BACK TO CLASS. WE MISS YOU.

                                          Love Ms Rain

Ms R   Ja 19, 1988
S____ wrk as mi i want to gv Litt Mong Abdul up adopsus
(*Social worker ask me if I want to give Little Mongo and Abdul up for adoption*)
I fel ki her
(*I feel kill her*)
Nnevr hep now wnt kiz way
(*Never help now want to take kids away*)
tsak Abdul i don notin
(*take Abdul I don't have nothing*)

Precious,

   It seems the opposite to me. If you keep Abdul you might have nothing. You are learning to read and write, that is everything.

   Come back to school when you get out the hospital.

You're only seventeen. Your whole life is in front of you.

Ms Rain

1/20
Gr____ cme vit sa onle dog dro babee an wak off
(*Grandmother come visit say only a dog will drop a baby and walk off*)
say lat no evn a dog
(*say later not <u>even</u> a dog*)

Dear Precious,
    Don't forget to put the year, '88, on your journal entries.
    Precious you are not a dog. You are a wonderful young woman who is trying to make something of her life. I have some questions for you:

1. Where was your grandmother when your father was abusing you?
2. Where is Little Mongo now?
3. What is going to be the best thing for you in this situation?

Ms Rain

Mss, Rinas
lot qu____ u ask   Hoo?
(*lot of questions you ask*)   (*Who?*)

PUSH

Nbi
(nobody)

aln
(alone)

no Frknm
(no Farrakhan)

no mmam
(no mama)

no gr____muver fther fucktz me yr
(no grandmother father fucks me years)

lii Mongl with my gr____
(Little Mongo with my grandmother)

bes four mi tostop breev i sm tim tik
(best for me to stop breathing I sometimes think)

aso i want to b god muvther
(also I wants to be good mother)

Precious Jones

Dear Dear Precious,

   Being a good mother might mean letting your baby be raised by someone who is better able than you to meet the child's needs.

Ms Rain

Mz Rain
Dan frget rite day Ms R
(Don't forget to write the date Ms Rain.)
I is be bt meet cldls ed.
(I is best able to meet my child's need.)

Ms Precious

73

Dear Ms Precious, 1/22/88

    When you are raising a small infant you need help. Who is going to help you? How will you support yourself? How will you keep learning to read and write?

Ms Rain

Ms Rain
th wfr hlp mma it help mi
(The welfare help Mama. It help me.)

Precious Mi

Dear Precious Miss,

    When you get home from the hospital look and see how much welfare has helped your mother.

    You could go further than your mother. You could get your G.E.D. and go to college. You could do anything Precious but you gotta believe it.

Love Blue Rain

Dear Blu
I lie tah nme Ms Ran. I ty ty
(I like that name Ms. Rain. I'm tired <u>tired</u>.)

Well I honestly did wanna jus' take Abdul home 'n rest so I could hurry up 'n go back to school. But when I git home from the hospital Mama try to kill me. I had told myself if she ever come at me like that again I will stab her to def. But when it happen, when she git up off that couch 'n charge toward me like fifty niggers, I ran. I just grab Abdul, my bags, 'n hit the door. I got new baby boy in my arms 'n she calling me bitch hoe slut say she gonna kill me 'cause I ruin her life. Gonna kill me wif her "BARE HANDS!" It's like a black wall gonna crash down on me, nuthin' to do but run. "First you steal my husband! Then you get me cut off welfare!" She MAD! No time to say nothin'. Once I'm outside the door I stop at top of the stairs, look hard at her. She still foaming at mouf, talking about her husband I spoze to steal. I do tell her one thing as I going down the stairs. I say, "Nigger rape me. I not steal shit fat bitch your husband RAPE me RAPE ME!"

I screaming holding little Abdul, hospital bag with Pampers 'n his stuff, 'n a shopping bag from Woolworth's with my stuff in it.

I don't even think, my feets just take me back to Harlem Hospital. You know Koch wanna close it, say niggers don't need no hospital all to theyself. Farrakhan say we need one. Miz Rain say Farrakhan is jive anti-Semitic, homophobe fool. My pussy hurt. I turn down piece of pavement lead to 'mergency. Then I turn back, go through front door, 'n say I wanna visit maternity ward. They not spozed to let you up without hassle 'cause of baby snatchers. But bitch see I got Abdul. She must know if anything I be dropping little homeboy off, not snatching nuffin'.

I get off elevator, looking for Nurse Lenore Harrison, that's Ms Butter's name from when I had Little Mongo. Done worked her way up to queen of the ward. What I gonna be, queen of babies? No, I gonna be queen of those ABCs—readin' 'n writin'. I not gonna stop going to school 'n I not going to give Abdul up and I is gonna get Little Mongo back one day, maybe. I hardly even know what she look like, aside from retarded, that is.

I'm waiting. 'Nother nurse pass me, look at me say she remember me from '83. She skinny, black, I don't remember her. She say she sorry to see me back here, had hoped I be done learned from my mistakes. What kinda shit is that! I didn't make no mistake unless it being born, 'n Miz Rain say I was born for a purpose, 'n Mr Wicher had said I had aptitude for maff. I don't know what purpose but I know I got a purpose, a reason, and according to Farrakhan I got a almighty allah god.

Mistake? I don't think so. Mistakes for niggers to rape. I think I might be the solution. Shit where nurse, yellow bitch. Ize homeless right now. Me 'n Abdul homeless. I can see evil Mama in room tearing posters off wall, messing up my clothes 'n shit. Well bitch gonna hafta get off her ass now!

Nurse Butter come. I tell her what happen. I tell her about school, 'bout Farrakhan 'n allah, 'bout maff— how Mr Wicher had told Mrs Lichenstein I got maff aptitude, and ABCs. How Miz Rain say I'm moving faster through the vowel 'n consonant sounds than even

Rita Romero, who is light skinned. I tell her I not hardly seed Little Mongo since my grandmother tooked her and how Abdul my daddy's baby too. I don't feel shamed—Carl Kenwood Jones freak NOT me!

I am Precious ABCDEFGHIJKLMNOPQRST
    UVWXYZ
My baby is born
My baby is black
I am girl
I am black
I want house to live

Help nurse, help me Miz Lenore. Help me. One thing from going to school 'n talking in class I done learned to talk up. Ms Rain say it's a big country. Say bombs cost more than welfare. Bombs to murder kids 'n shit. Guns to war people—all that cost more than milk 'n Pampers. Say no shame. No shame. Most time it seem like hype, 'cause she say it so much. But that why she say she say it—to reprogram us to love ourselve. I love me. I ain' gonna let that big fat bitch kick my ass 'n shout on me. And I ain' giving Abdul away. And I ain' gonna stop school.

Nurse Butter saying she going off duty now, hate to leave me but got to pick up her daughter from babysitter, nurse coming on duty will help me.

I ask new nurse for sanitary napkin, I'm bleeding. This nurse I don't know. She look me kinda cold. She whisper talk some shit to another nurse then come tell me I got to go to the armory. It's like they tired. I'm a problem got to be got out they face. I ain' got no coat, I say. They say people at shelter give me something when I get there. Sit still, van gonna come git me and drop me, and some of the other patients, off. Nurse say lots of people get out hospital wif no place to go, calm down, you not so special.

The armory is like a dungeon of bricks, damp, wif a few 'lectrik lightbulbs hanging from ceiling. A bitch in bed next to bed I'm in hit herself over 'n over in mouf with her own fist. Over 'n OVER. Another girl with swole junkie hands, sores, and shit say, "Put your bags *in* bed with you."

I'm bress feeding Abdul. He cry. He wet. He seem like little rat or cat. I know some things to do for him but I get scared when he cough throw up. He is only seven days old. He could die. Woman, big woman, bigger than me and old—she around forty, come up 'n snatch blanket off my cot. Remind me of Mama, the red light in her eye, the way her hair stick up. What I'm spozed to do; my pussy feel torn apart in pieces, my lower back pain me, my bresses is leaking milk, my bra wet and not smell nice, and maniac done snatched my blanket.

"Give the kid back her blanket," lady wif junkie sores on her arm say.

"Fuck you," maniac say, "I ain' giving back shit."

I jus' take off sheet that's on top the plastic-covered mattress and wrap it around Abdul, then I wrap myself around Abdul and hunker down on that cold plastic. I wish they would turn the lights out. But they don't. I go to sleep anyway. When I wake up bags with my stuff gone, one of my shoes the laces is untied. Maybe that's what wake me up, them trying to get the shoes off my feet. How many days I lay up in Mama's house thinking nothing could be worse than that. I get up, tie my shoes. These bitches here crazy. I feed Abdul. My body is his breakfast. I gotta get something to eat myself.

I'm at armory not far from hospital. This shit ain' gonna work. What time is it? Six a.m. Miz West! Live down the hall from us, stop Mama from kicking me to death when Mongo being born. She like me. I always did go to the store for her since I was little.

"Precious, bring me back a pack of Winstons and a big bag of pork rinds."

"Yes Miz West."

"Keep the change Precious."

One time she tell me, You ever wanna talk about anything you could come to me.

But I never did. And I don't know her phone number now. How would she get in Mama's house to get my stuff out anyway?

"Breakfast?" dope addict girl say.

"Yeah," I say. Lots of the girlz, womens, is moving toward a door. Some just sit on the bed cots like they in shock or some shit. Dope addict girl point at people moving, say follow them. I do.

Coffee out a steel pitcher, a little box of cornflakes, and a banana. I don't drink coffee. It's almost 7 o'clock.

Fuck it, I go wait for Ms Rain in lobby. Maybe it be one of those days she come in early. I wait there till 8:45 a.m. She is shock when she walk through door and see me sitting on floor of lobby in Hotel Theresa wif Abdul in my arms. I almost forgit about me for a minute, I feel so sorry for her. She just ABC teacher, not no social worker or shit. But where else can I go?

I can tell by Ms Rain's face I'm not gonna be homeless no more. She mumbling cursing about *what* damn safety net, most basic needs, a newborn child, *A NEW-BORN CHILD!* She going OFF now. Rhonda come in behind her. No class, all of Each One Teach One is on the phone! They calling everybody from Mama to the mayor's office to TV stations! Before this day is up, Ms Rain say, you gonna be living somewhere, as god is my witness. As GOD is my witness!

Thas when Queens shit come up. They wanna send me to ½way house in Queens, immediate opening! NO! What I know about Queens?! They got Arabs, Koreans, Jews, and Jamaicans—all kinda shit me and Abdul don't need to be bothered with. Here, I stay here in Harlem. Harlem house say they couldn't take me for two weeks. Ms Rain's boss git on phone. She is West Indian woman, don't take no shit. Boyfriend sit on some council. She hang up phone, say, They can take her tomorrow. So they just have to find me a place for tonight. Everyone says I can stay over their house. But you know where I stay? Ms Rain got friend who is caretaker or something at Langston Hughes' house which is not but around the corner, it's city landmark. I SPEND ONE NIGHT IN LANGSTON HUGHES' HOUSE HE USED TO LIVE IN. Me and Abdul in the Dream Keeper's house! Day after that, we come here, where I been ever since. Here, at Advancement House, main good thing is they got somebody we can trust to take care of our babies while we go to school for four hours a day, three times a week. Queens, no Ms Rain, no school.

I like my room here. Better than home, Mama's house, I mean. I got bed for me, crib for Abdul. Dresser drawers, desk, chair, bookcase for my books and Abdul's books. Some of my books is:

1. *The Life of Lucy Fern* 1 and 2 (it's two books) by Moira Crone
2. *Pat King's Family* by Karen McFall
3. *Harriet Tubman: Conductor on the Underground Railroad* by Ann Petry
4. *Wanted Dead or Alive: The True Story of Harriet Tubman* by Ann McGovern (got *two* Harriet books!)
5. *Malcolm X* by Arnold Adoff
6. *A Piece of Mine* by J. California Cooper
7. *The Color Purple* by Alice Walker
8. *Selected Poems* by Langston Hughes

some books Abdul got:

1. *The Black BC's* by Lucille Clifton
2. *Harold and the Purple Crayon* by Crockett Johnson

3. *The Story of a Little Mouse Trapped in a Book*
   by Monique Felix
4. *The Boy Who Didn't Believe in Spring* by
   Lucille Clifton
5. *Hi, Cat!* by Ezra Jack Keats

Most of what we got Ms Rain give us. I would like a job, a paycheck—be able to buy what I want when I want it.

We reading *The Color Purple* in school. Which is really hard for me. Ms Rain try to break it down but most of it I can't read myself. But the rest of the class kinda can, 'cept Rita. But how Ms Rain hook it up I am getting something out the story. I cry cry *cry* you hear me, it sound in a way so much like myself except I ain' no butch like Celie. But just when I go to break on that shit, go to tell class what Five Percenters 'n Farrakhan got to say about butches, Ms Rain tell me I don't like homosexuals she guess I don't like her 'cause she one. I was shocked as shit. Then I jus' shut up. Too bad about Farrakhan. I still believe allah and stuff. I guess I still believe everything. Ms Rain say homos not who rape me, not homos who let me sit up not learn for sixteen years, not homos who sell crack fuck Harlem. It's true. Ms Rain the one who put the chalk in my hand, make me queen of the ABCs.

Oh, I not tell you that! Every year mayor's office give awards to outstanding students in literacy pro-

grams. Well, this year, 1988, it was me. After I get in
½way house (which turn out to be only ½way cool 'cause
some of the bitches there is Sick with a capital *S* (capital letter is how you start off sentence or say something
with deep shit meaning like Fuck with capital *F* you
mad or some shit like that!). But like I said the good
thing, the real good thing, about ½way house is it in
Harlem so I could keep going to school easy.

So anyway by February I'm pretty settled in
Advancement House. So I work all spring, memorizing
letter sounds, writing in journal, reading books. I have
read *Pat King's Family* 'bout white woman whose husband abuse 'n abandon her. I have read *Ain Nobodi Gon'
Turn Me 'Round* 'bout civil rights. I ain' know black people in this country went through shit like that. But thas
the deal here in cracker jack city as Farrakhan say. So
anyway I made so much progress I won award. Literacy
Award. I get it September of 1988. Ms Rain wanted to
give it to me even before then. She say she had wanted
to give it to me after I come back from Abdul being
born and homeless 'n stuff. But director say, Well, we
got other students who deserve it, let's see if Precious
got staying power.

So I get award from mayor's office, money ($75) from
Each One Teach One, and class have a party for me.

Things going good in my life, almost like *The Color
Purple*. Abdul nine months old, *walking*! Smart smart.
He smart. I been reading to him since day he was born
damn near. I love *The Color Purple*, that book give me so

much strength. Ms Rain say a group of black men wanted to stop movie from the book. Say unfair picture of nigger men. She ax me what do *I* think. Unfair picture? Unfortunately it a picture I know, except of course Farrakhan who is real man. But I never seen him 'cept on videos! He say problem is not crack but the cracker! I go for that shit.

Ms Rain say one of the critcizsm of *The Color Purple* is it have fairy tale ending. I would say, well shit like that can be true. Life can work out for the best sometimes. Ms Rain love *Color Purple* too but say realism has its virtues too. Izm, smizm! Sometimes I wanna tell Ms Rain shut up with all the IZM stuff. But she my teacher so I don't tell her shut up. I don't know what "realism" mean but I do know what REALITY is and it's a mutherfucker, lemme tell you.

Mama come to ½way house. (What is ½way house? I thought I already told you. But anyway I tell you from book I read about battered woman. In a way I was a battered woman but I was not a woman—actually I was a chile. And it wasn't my husband. I don't have a husband. It was my muver.) But anyway, I never readed no book about a place for children, jus' for grown-up women (in a way I am that too) and babies. But this book I was reading was about a woman who got beat up by her husband. And she escape to ½way house. She asks people at the place just what ½way house is. They tell her, You is ½way between the life you had and the life you want to have. Ain't that nice. You should read that book if you have a chance.

So I'm in ½way house, I been there, oh, not quite a year; like in book I read—I'm on threshold of stepping out into my new life, an apartment for me, Abdul, and maybe Little Mongo, we see on that one, mo' education, new friends. I done left Mama, Daddy, Ms Lichenstein, I.S. 146 behind. So I'm wondering what hoe want wif me. Can't get no money. I went see about Little Mongo back when I first get in Advancement House. They put her in institution, say she severely (mean real) retarded, and Toosie hadn't been doing things that would help her—like colors on the wall and books 'n shit, so she really in bad shape. They say even if she could be help, take a lot more than me to help, and ain't I got full load with Abdul.

Anyway live-in social worker at Advancement House call me into office, say, Precious, your mother is here to see you. Ax me do I want to see her. I say OK. (It's not like I *want* to see her but since she comed all this way here I will see her. She know better, I think, than to fuck wif me now.)

I walk in dayroom. Mama quiet. Mama look bad, don't have to get close to know she smell bad. But then I look Mama and see my face, my body, my color—we bofe big, dark. Am I ugly? Is Mama ugly? I'm not sure. I know she got pussy odor and ugly brogan shoes like people make fun of and giant green dress that her legs come out of like black jelly elephant legs. I'm ashamed, this is my Mama. No matter how fly my braids is, how I grease my skin, scalp, no matter how many jew'ries, this is my mother.

Mama don't look me in eye. She never did 'less she was shouting on me or telling me what to do—cook her something or go to store. She look down say, "Your daddy dead." She come out the house to tell me that! So what! I'm glad the nigger's dead. No, I don't mean that, but so what. Mama quiet. Mama say, "Carl had the AIDS virus."

You know, so what, why you telling me. Then oh! No! Oh no, I get all squozen inside. Carl fuckes me. I could be done have it. Abdul could be—oh no, I can't even say nuffin'.

A long time I don't say nuffin', jus' look at Mama. This what I come out of? Like Abdul and Little Mongo come out of me. If she ever said a kind word to me I don't remember it. Sixteen years I live in her house without knowing how to read. Since I was little her husband fuck me beat me. My daddy. I want to hate him—but it's funny I, he, give me the only good thing in my life aside from Ms Rain, ABCs, and girls at school; Abdul come from him, my son, my brother. But Mama give me to him. This my mother. Carl come in the night, take food, what money they is, fuck us bofe. Something cross my mind now. Man rape Celie turn out not to be her daddy.

"Mama?"

She look over where I'm at.

"Yo' huzbn, Carl, my real daddy?" I ask.

"What chu mean?"

"Carl, was he my real daddy? Was you married to him for real?"

"He your daddy, couldn't no one else be your daddy. I was with him since since I was sixteen. I never been with nobody else. We not married though, he got a wife though, a real wife, purty light-skin woman he got two kids by."

Hmmm, they got special kinda AIDS for yellow bitches? Mama! Thought jus' now hit me, don't know why, it the most obvious—do Mama got it?

"You got it?" I ask.

"No."

"How you know?"

"We never did, you know—"

I look at Mama like she fucking crazy! What she talking about?

"You know," she repeat. "What you got to do to get it."

"He never fuck you," I say shock.

"Oh yeah," she say. "But not like faggots, in the ass and all, so I know—"

Her voice trail off, stupid bitch. I'm jus' staring at her. I wanna kill her. I remember what I know from AIDS Awareness Day at school. Look at Mama, say, "You better get tested."

That's all really I got to say. Mama look at me like she wanna say something.

"You welcome back home," she say.

"I home here," I say. Silence. "Well I guess I better go see 'bout Abdul 'n do homework." Mama don't move. So, you know, I jus' get up and leave.

Song playing in my head now, not rap. Not TV colors flashing funny noise pictures in on me, scratching and itching in my brain at the same time. I see a color I don't know the name for, maybe one like only another kind of animal thas not human can see. Like butterflies? I ask Ms Rain tomorrow do butterflies see colors. Song caught on me like how plastic bags on tree branches. I sit on my bed. New picture on wall now. I got Alice Walker up there with Harriet Tubman 'n Farrakhan. But she can't help me now. Where my *Color Purple*? Where my god most high? Where my king? Where my black love? Where my man love? Woman love? Any kinda love? Why me? I don't deserve this. I not crack addict. Why I get Mama for a mama? Why I not born a light-skin dream? Why? Why? It's a movie, splashing like swimming pool at Y, in my head. I see Abdul running away from me, he is like little animal running toward a cliff, I am running running too, all over is clowns with evil eyes laffing at me I can't run fast enuff, the music is playing louder now I going off cliff myself now, maybe I don't come back. Don't see Abdul. A huh! A Huh! I can't breathe! Song loud now real loud. I stop running. It's grass green all aroun'. I listen to song, I can hear it now. It's Aretha. I always did wish she was my mother or Miss Rain or Tina Turner; a mother I be proud of, love me. I breathe in, lay down on my bed. Bed, I remember, I finded for myself when Mama go off on me that last time. Aretha singing, "Gotta find me an angel gotta find me an angel in my liifffe."

Heart hurt. I don't know what to do. If not for Abdul (name mean servant of god) I . . . I . . . my god, Jezus— allah most high, ABDUL! Mama, Carl, me, Abdul Abdul Abdul, he my angel, my little angel. Do Abdul got it?

I don't know what to do. I ask Ms Rain tomorrow.

On the wall under pictures of Harriet, Alice Walker, and Farrakhan is my Literacy Award. That is good proof to me I can do anything. Already Abdul know ABC. Plus he know his numbers. Barely talk and he counting. I did that. One day I going back for Little Mongo. Maybe I make the day sooner than I had thought. Time, I want to learn to look at round clock and tell time. No one ever show me. I never tell Ms Rain I don't know that. Got everything like digital watch display, them watches from Korea. What's the difference between Korean and Jap? Mr Wicher say I got aptitude for maff. Where I gonna go when I leave ½way house? I got AIDS? HIV? What's the difference? My son got it? Lil Mongo? How I gonna learn and be smart if I got the virus? Why me? Why me? Maybe virus don't get me? Maybe, I, jus' 'cause Carl have it don't mean me and Abdul have it.

I gotta go upstairs to the nursery to get Abdul. I think about this later. It make me feel stupid crazy, I mean stupid crazy.

I don't say nuffin' Monday in school, Ms Rain ax me what wrong. I say, I OK, talk about it later. Ms Rain say what about now. I write her in my journal book.

Jan 9, 1989

One yr I ben scool I like scool I love my techr
(*One year I been school I like school I love my teacher*)
lot i lern. Books I read, chile care work comprts
(*lot I learn. Books I read, child care, work computers*)
Ms Rain i wood like to get a gud job lern wrk comptrs
(*Ms Rain I would like to get a good job learn work computers*)
get apt me n lil Mongo and Abdul
(*get apartment me and Little Mongo and Abdul*)
Ms Rain I ass you wy Me?
(*Ms Rain I ask you why Me?*)

                                        Precious

Dear Ms Precious,

You make my day! You don't just don't know how much I love having you in class, how much

PUSH

I love you period. And I am proud of you; the
whole school is proud of you.

   I'm sure you'll be able to find a job when you
get your G.E.D. And maybe your social worker
could help you get a nice place for you, Little
Mongo, and Abdul.

   I don't know what you mean by your question,
"Why me?" Please explain.

Ms Rain 1/9/89

Blue,
   So many time u say i cood call you bi yr firs
name. I nver doo.
   (*So many time you say I could call you by your first
name. I never do.*)

<blockquote>
Blu Ran

Blue RAIN

Rain

is gr_____
   (*gray*)

but saty
   (*stay*)

my rain
</blockquote>

A pome
(*a poem*)
that all i hav to say rit now

1/11/89
Precious Jones
the poet

91

1/13/89
I talk to s____ wrk tody she gonn get tess for me
(*I talk to social worker today she gonna get test for me*)

an Abdul (se____ of God) to see
(*and Abdul (servant of God) to see*)
see the i
ey see
(*eye*)

see me
liv
(*live*)

or

die
poslv
(*positive*)

or

negv
(*negative*)
wh? wh?
(*why? why?*)
must
I li
(*lie*)
to misel
(*myself*)
I
must

PUSH

no
(*know*)
the truf
(*truth*)

Precious P. Jones

1/13/89
Dear Precious POET Jones!
    Awesome! I love your poetry and your
drawings. What are you and Abdul going to see?
    How did you like the poems we read in class?
Love Ms Blue Rain

Ms Rain
Mi an Abdul got a scrit
(*Me and Abdul got a secret*)
I tell yo latr promois
(*I tell you later promise*)
no i tell yo now
IV HIV HIV U an Mi coold hav HIV
(*IV HIV HIV You and me could have HIV*)
mi sun God Allh
(*my son God Allah*)
Alice Walk pra o IV VI YWXYZ
(*Alice Walker pray oh IV VI YWXYZ*)
I ah V I I H IH I HIV
HIV.

Precious P. Jones

Dear Precious,   1/23/89
     Are you saying you and Abdul need to take
an HIV test? Well, tell me as much as you feel
comfortable.

                                   Ms Rain

Blue wmon
who tech mi who hep mi I don no whut
(*who teach me who help me I don't know what*)

to sa it hard to xplxn i nver tel mi hole store. Yes I
(*to say it hard to explain I never tell my whole story. Yes I*)

need tess four AID I skred thas ALL four nov
(*need test for AIDS. I scared that's ALL for now*)

                                   pane
                                   (*pain*)
                              Precious Pane
                                   (*Pain*)
                              2/1/89

I gotta learn more than ABCs now. I got to learn more
than read write, this big BIG. This the biggest thing
happen to Precious P. Jones in her life. I got the AIDS
virus. Thas what tess say. We sitting in circle thas
when I tell class. Jus' like it's cornflakes for breakfast.
After so many days looking out the window, doing
double talk in my journal. I just come out and say it.
     "Nurse at clinic say to me, You are HIV positive," I

say to girls, we sit in circle, some faces new, some the same faces from first day—Rita Romero, she hanged. Jermaine still here, Consuelo gone. Rhonda still on set, some new girls—who is like me when I first walk through the door. Only now I the one who say "keep on keepin' on!" to new girls. I show them how the dialogue journal work. You know how you write to teacher 'n she write back to you in the same journal book like you talkin' on paper and you could SEE your talk coming back to you when the teacher answer you back. I mean thas what had made me really like writing in the beginning, knowing my teacher gonna write me back when I talk to her. I explain the phonics game, vocab building list—all stuff like that *I* know now. We have a class project—LIFE STORY. It's where we write our life stories and put it all in one big book. From the girls who been here awhile I only one ain' done my story yet. One day when I have time I read you what the other girls wrote. Some bitches get down, some bullshit. When I hear Rhonda's story, Rita Romero's story, I know I not the worse off. Rita's daddy kill her mother in front her eyes. Rita been on street selling pussy since she was twelve. She the only one came in like me—can't read, write nothin'. Then Rhonda's brother raping her since she was a chile, her mother fine out and put Rhonda, not brother, out. Consuelo in fantasy land, she pretty, long hair. But I glad she gone. She wave her pretty in my face like a flag, tell me exercise and stay out sun so I don't get no darker. Say she found good man.

I glad. I don't hate no one. I don't hate Mama, Carl, so why I gonna get bent outta shape behind some Spanish talking bitch who bent outta shape 'cause she dark like nigger instead of white. Shit, Rhonda a nigger and she lighter than Consuelo! Consuelo did leave but Jermaine didn't follow behin' her. Jermaine stayed on. She write real in book. Call what she is sexual preference. Say she shouldn't be judge 'cause of that. She got hard rock story too. Say mens beat her for what she is. Mother put her out house when she fine out.

These girlz is my friends. I been like the baby in a way 'cause I was only 16 first day I walk in. They visit at hospital when I had Abdul and take up a collection when Mama kick me out and bring stuff to ½way house for me—clothes, cassette player, tuna fish, and Cambull soup, and stuff. They and Ms Rain is my friends and family.

Ms Rain a butch. This still shock to me 'cause you can not tell it, but I remember what she said—not homos who rape me, not homos who let me be ignerent. I forgets all that ol' shit lately—Five Percenters, Black Israelites, etc etc (etc etc mean yeah yeah). I never be butch like Celie but it don't make me happy—make me sad. Maybe I never find no love, nobody. At least when I look at the girls I see *them* and when they look they see *ME*, not what I looks like. But it seems like boyz just see what you looks like. A boy come out my pussy. Was nothing. A dark spot in the sky; then turn to life in me. When he grow up he gonna laff big black girls? He gon' laff at dark skin like he got? One thing I say about Farrakhan and Alice Walker they help me like being black. I wish I wasn't fat but I am. Maybe one day I like that too, who knows.

But I look my friends in the circle and I tell them, test say I'm HIV positive. And all the tongues dead, can't talk no more. Rita Romero hug me like I'm her chile and I cry and Ms Rain rub my back and say let it out, Precious, let it out. I cry for every day of my life. I cry for Mama what kinda story Mama got to do me like she do? And I cry for my son, the song in my life. The little brown penis, booty, fat thighs, roun' eyes, the voice of love say, Mama, Mama he call me.

Then crying stop. Rita go to her purse and get magazine call *Body Positive* say I got to join HIV community. Jezus! It's a community of them? Us, I mean. But I tell her, Not now. I just need to think. Is life a hammer to beat me down? Jermaine jump up do boxing dance (she think she Mike Tyson!) say fight back! I laugh, a little.

Ms Rain say we got to write now in our journals. Say each of our lives is important. She got us book from Audre Lorde, a writer woman like Alice Walker. Say each of us has a story to tell. What is a black unicorn? I don't really understand the poem but I like it.

I don't have nothing to write today—maybe never. Hammer in my heart now, beating me, I feel like my blood a giant river swell up inside me and I'm drowning. My head all dark inside. Feel like giant river I never cross in front me now. Ms Rain say, You not writing

Precious. I say I drownin' in river. She don't look me like I'm crazy but say, If you just sit there the river gonna rise up drown you! Writing could be the boat carry you to the other side. One time in your journal you told me you had never really told your story. I think telling your story git you over that river Precious.

I still don't move. She say, "Write." I tell her, "I am tired. Fuck you!" I scream, "You don't know nuffin' what I been through!" I scream at Ms Rain. I never do that before. Class look shock. I feel embarrass, stupid; sit down, I'm made a fool of myself on top of everything else. "Open your notebook Precious." "I'm tired," I says. She says, "I know you are but you can't stop now Precious, you gotta push." And I do.

IV

2/27/89

Ms Rain say more now, much more. She wan more from me. More than 15 minutes an she write back. Say walk wif it. The *journal*? I say. Yeah, she say, Walk wif da journl. Everywhere you go, ~~journl~~ journal go. You know I go walk with Abdul etc., take journal, write stuff in journal.

learnin lot: to too two. three diffrent 2 words. Each one is ~~diffrent~~ different. Four for fore. Three four words.

Stori

Ms Rain tell me to <u>koncentrate</u> on my story. When I ~~ka~~ can not spell a word Ms Rain tell me sound out firs lettr c____ and draw a lin. Thas concentrate. Latrer she will fill in rite spelling for me.

But my spelling is impruv. Way way improve.

Ms Rain say I seem dpress
depr<u>ssion</u> is she say ang<u>rer</u> turn in.

Jermaine say not <u>necessarily</u> rally
(Whutevr Ms Rain say Jermaine don agree)

Rite wRite write
more she say
talk more
    say ~~gte~~ get ½ hos staf to get babee sitter xtra
hr so I can go to meatings, movie.
    You no I never (good spell) bin a movie, cep
vidios on Mama's VCR. I never bin chuc. Rhonda
goe ALL the time. Want take me an Ms Rain.
She want take hole skool sins she bin savd.

For
a monf it bin like this. I feel daze.
Ms Rain see it
    say you not same girl i kno.
    is tru. I am a difrent
    persn
    anybuddy wood be don't u think?
    dont
    u
    think.

Ms Rain
    say go back back back
    far
    you

can rember.
what four? I say
whut i got to rmember i nevr dun forgit
mama daddy scool
Y why go thru ALL (i like that word) DAT
ALL DAT
ALL DAT
SHIT
But Ms Rain
worryed worryed worr<u>ied</u> about mi.

Thas nice sumebuddy care but I don want to
worri her. She sen note ½way hous for me to cum
scool ½ hr erly to write. And go downtown wif
Rhonda for insect talk grup and chuc. I think I
AM
MAD.
ANGERREEY   angerry
                   very
                   mi life
                   not good
                   i got dizeez. Ms Rain
                   say NOT dizeez
                   I say whut is it then.
                   I Talk
                   angr
                   to Ms Rain
she say u <u>no</u>tice yr spelin <u>ch</u>ange wen yu hav
feelins not tal bout in book she say i am nt dyslx
nune that say its emoshunal disturb lets talk bout it

I was fine til HIV thing
she say i still fine
but prblm not jus HIV it mama Dady
BUT I was gon dem
I escap dem like Harriet
Ms Ran say we can nt escap the pass.
the way free is hard
look Harriet H-A-R-R-I-E-T
i pratise her name.
Rita say keep tinkin whut you got to bee
thankfill for
Jermaine (she bes writer in skool) say semicoln
no coln
go befour list
:
i gt two bee thankfill four:
Ms Rain
~~scool~~ school
girlz in class
Abdul
Toosday Rita take me VILLAG
Sat we go muzeum

sun day chuch
MONDY we gonna read Harriet T. book

I feel btretter 😊 glad I write my book

                                        Precious

PUSH

3/6/89

Wat it be like to bee in luv. I wondr this al the time ALL time all the time.

I kno sex sex so much. I kno bout sex alot a lot wht it be like to hav a fren, thas a guy I mean.

I GOT frens.

I don't sho Ms Rain everything in my book no mor. she mi techer Don want her kno if I rite about SEX if I have sex wif a kute coot boy thas my own age I wil ____.

Rita got a man. Rhonda God. Ms Rain a fren. Jermaine say hole worl her lovr.

3/8/89

My favrt thing to take Abdul down to nursery at breakfus
then
not eat breakfus. n that giv me time
to
wallk throo Harlem in
mornin to school
mostly pepul goin
to work
faces faces
iron brown
black glas
tears
not jazzee
Harlem

of Langston Huges
Harlmen Poet Laureeyet!
this
a Harlem done
took
a beating
but
mornin
if you
like
me
you see
ILANATHA tree rape
concreet
n birf
spiky green
trunk
life.
see
mens in
vaykent lot bild
fire
lik indiens
shar
whut
they got.
Bus
roll
mostlee wmen

PUSH

downtwn
sky opn
blu legs
for
sun.

    I hit 116th n sometimes I walk up Madison
and go aroun the park, the park nevr clean but
green. Pas bafhouse. Bafhouse where faggits
meet nekkid fuck each other. I wondr wat that be
like. trees. after park liberry on 124th. I got libry
card. Nex door libry is none house. Nones live
ther serve god don fuck. Rhonda say you go in
basement where nones live is babee bones. Rita
say das a lie. She Kathlic. I say God. Sho me god.
Keep going down 124th vaykent lot.

       i stop. Gon rite bout vaykent lot.
       uuuuuuugh dog shit dog shit
          crummel up briks
          steell fence
          lifes of trash
          cancer yr eye
          multiply
          ugliness
          greazee shit
          garbage cans, rottin
          cloze PAMPER filthee

       dope addicks
       pile up
       flow ovr
       uglee
       I HATE
       HATE
       UGLY

turn from vaykent lot n is vaykent pepul with
kraters like what u see wen you look at spots on
the moon. wen you see moon on space movies is
holes on it, kraters. thas on dope addicts arms—
kraters. Dese not crack addicts like on one-two-
six. Dese people on 1-2-4 is HAIRRUN shuters.
There eyez is like far away space ships. they don
see you, only smell pepul go buy for money.
They money dogs. If they sniff money they will
try to take it. I guess. Thas whut I always here.
I nevr reely had a dope addict hurt me. We hate
dope addicts. We, me, norml pepul. I git confuse
how i git wif dope addicts. How whut they got
I got. I don unnerstan DOPE. Whut I see do
not look like fun. it look SAD. It look teef fall
out. they have gums not teef, talk funny, walk
stupid. WHY? If I stay on 124th to 7th Ave more
vaykent lot. Maybee pass nigger wif needle in
his arm noddin in the wind. Drops of blood
drip down. maybe pass sex sicko wif peniss out,

flashlite eyes shine sperms on you. Its a block
like a fog wif worms. the pepul worms. I hate em.
UGLY.

But confuse.

Across from bar on Lenox btween 124 n 125
is only zerox shop in Harlm. blak sister and dater
own it. when zerox at school break down I cum
there git zerox. in shop she got books, cards, blak
stuff I hardley ever have money to buy stuff. I
DIE for I steel. Nver will Precious Jones steel (no
more) or shute dope.

Thas whut tv sho, niggers steel shute dope
steel shute dope harlm crime crime. On top bar
is Diane McIntyre's skool. I wood hav liked to
go to dancin scool when I was young. Its too late
now. I'm eighteen. An Abdul a boy. Boyz don go
Only faggit boyz. I don want Abdul to be faggit
or dope addick.

But what I confuse about is this. Itz so uglee
dope addicks—dey teef, dey underwater walkin,
steelin. Spred AIDS an heptietis.

But Rita was one of dese pepul an she is
GOOD. I luv her.

When I get to school early sometimes I just sit in front
part on the black plastic couch that need tape where it
cut and the yellow foam pads show through. School

start at 9 o'clock. The secretary get here at 8:00 a.m. I don' get here before that 'cause the door locked and I would have to wait in the lobby downstairs. Which I don't like.

Our room is nice. Nicer since we have one day where we come in "raggedy" and bring our own cleaning stuff 'n posters, pictures, 'n plants from home 'n fix up our room. Ms Rain say bring something of YOU! I bring picture of Abdul and plant from Woolworth on 125th Street. It growed. Leaves big. Ms Rain done changed its pot three times.

Ms Rain get here 'bout 8:15 or so, usually right behind or in front of Rita or Rhonda. They bofe erly birds too. Ms Rain jus' give whoever here the keys from her purse to open up our classroom while she do whatever she do—fix coffee, git books from supply room—stuff like that. By 8:30 a.m. early birds good to go! Room quiet sunny. We just open our notebook, Ms Rain usually say something like, You got 10 or 15 minutes 'fore the "rabble" get here. Yeah, I don't know exactly what is the rabble. She jus' joking for Jermaine and them who hit the door roun' 9:05 a.m. Always a little late, always complaining 'bout something—the weather, train, what the newspaper say.

Me, I, just look at the sun coming in through the front window. Pretty soon it move around and come in through the side window. I like the routine of school, the dream of school. I wonder where I be if I had been learning all those years I sit at I.S. 146. Favorite book?

Maybe it's our book, the big book with all our stories in it. Not mine yet. I'm just putting stuff in my journal now.

Telling time is *easy*. Fractions, percents, multiplying, dividing is EASY. Why no one never taught me these things before. Rita say, All people with HIV or AIDS is innocent victims; it's a disease, not a "good," a "bad." You know what she mean? Well, thas good 'cause I don't. I cannot see how I am the same as a white faggit or crack addict. Rita kiss my forehead, hold each my cheeks with her hands, look me in my eyes, "Negra," she say, her eyes big like babies', black black eyes. "You don't see now but will. You will."

I don't know how I will, I don't even know what she's talkin' about. She's talking about *Life*, Ms Rain say. Well, I don't know what life is all about either. I know I'm eighteen, magic number. And my reading score is 2.8. I ask Ms Rain what that mean. She say it's a number! And can't no numbers measure how far I done come in jus' two years. She say forget about the numbers and just keep working. The author has a message and the reader's job is to decode that message as thoroughly as possible. A good reader is like a detective, she say, looking for clues in the text. A good reader is like you Precious, she say. Passionate! Passionately involved with whut they are reading. Don't worry about numbers and fill in the blank, just read and write!

I'm changing. Things I don't care about no more:

if boyz love me
extensions
new clozes

what I care about is:

STAYING HEALTHY
sex (____)
notebook, writing poems

Ms Rain say don't always rhyme, stretch for words to fall like drops of rain, snowflakes—did you know no two snowflakes is alike? Have you ever seen a snowflake? I haven't! All I seen is gobs of dirty gray shit. You mean to tell me that nasty stuff is made of snowy flakes. I don't believe it.

Each day is different. All the days is gobbed together to make a year, all the years gobbed together to make a life. I have a secret. Secret is, I mean I think Rita and Ms Rain halfway know but they too nice to get any further in my business than I want them in. I mean I have kids. But I never have a guy, you know like that. It never usta be on my mind. All I want before is Daddy get the fuck off me! But now I think about *that*, you know, that being fucking a cute boy. I think about that and I think about being a poet or rapper or an artist even. It's this guy on one-two-five, Franco, he done painted pictures on the steel gates that's over almos' all the store windows. At night you walk down and each one is painted different. I like that better than museum.

PUSH

It's so many different ways to walk the few blocks
home. Turn a corner and you see all different. Pass 116th
'n Lenox, more abandoned land, buildings falling down.
How it git so ugly is people throw trash all in it. City
don't pick it up; dogs doo doo. Peoples wif no bafroom
piss 'n shit. Ugliness grow multiplied by ten. Keep
walkin' down Lenox to one-twelve you pass projects. I
never did live in projects. I live in 444 Lenox Avenue
almost all my life. Where I live before that house I don't
know, maybe wif my grandmother.

Wonder about Mama sometimes. Wonder about
Carl more. Carl Kenwood Jones. I got session wif counselor today. Last week we try to figure out how long I
been infected. People at retard place say Lil Mongo
don't got it. She say that could mean Daddy get AIDS
pretty fast from time he first infected to time he die?
'Cause if Lil Mongo don't got it maybe he didn't have it
1983 when she born. Then after she born he go away a
long time. So maybe I get it eighty-six, eighty-seven?
Counselor say, I'm on top now. I'm young, is got no disease and stuff, not no drug addict. I could live a long
time, she say. I ask her what's a long time. She don't say.

I think some of the girls at Advancement House
know I am . . . am *positive*. I mean wifout trying I know
some of they bizness. They never was too friendly; since
Mama come wif her news, they even less friendly. But
who cares? I'm not tight wif these girls in the house.
These bitches got problems, come in room and steal
shit. I know I ain' the only one that got it, even though

that's how it feels. But I'm probably the only one get it from they daddy. Counselor, Ms Weiss, say she try to find out as much about Daddy for me as she can.

How much I want to know? And for what? I tell counselor I can't talk about Daddy now. My clit swell up I think Daddy. Daddy sick me, *disgust* me, but still he sex me up. I nawshus in my stomach but hot tight in my twat and I think I want it back, the smell of the bedroom, the hurt—he slap my face till it sting and my ears sing separate songs from each other, call me names, pump my pussy in out in out in out awww I come. He bite me *hard*. A hump! He slam his hips into me HARD. I scream pain he come. He slap my thighs like cowboys do horses on TV. Shiver. Orgasm in me, his body shaking, grab me, call me Fat Mama, Big Hole! You LOVE it! Say you love it! I wanna say I DON'T. I wanna say I'm a chile. But my pussy popping like grease in frying pan. He slam in me again. His dick soft. He start sucking my tittie.

I wait for him get off me. Lay there stare at wall till wall is a movie, *Wizard of Oz*, I can make that one play anytime. Michael Jackson, scarecrow. Then my body take me over again, like shocks after earthquake, shiver me, I come again. My body not mine, I hate it coming.

Afterward I go bafroom. I smear shit on my face. Feel good. Don't know why but it do. I never tell nobody about that before. But I would do that. If I go to insect support group what will I hear from other girls. I bite my fingernails till they look like disease, pull strips of my skin away. Get Daddy's razor out cabinet. Cut cut cut arm wrist, not trying to die, trying to plug myself back in. I am a TV set wif no picture. I am broke wif no mind. No past or present time. Only the movies of being someone else. Someone not fat, dark skin, short hair, someone not fucked. A pink virgin girl. A girl like Janet Jackson, a sexy girl don't no one get to fuck. A girl for value. A girl wif little titties whose self is luvlee just Luv-Vell-LEE!

I hate myself when I think Carl Kenwood Jones. Hate wif a capital letter. Counselor say, "Memories." How is something a memory if you never forgit? But I push it to the corner of my brain.

I exhausted, I mean wipe out! What kinda chile gotta think about a daddy like I do? But I'm not a chile. I'm a mother of a chile myself!

In school we had to memorize a poem like the rappers do. And say it in front the class. Everybody do real short poems except me and Jermaine. She do poem by lady name Pat Parker. I get up to do my poem, it's by Langston Hughes, I dedicate it to Abdul. Introduce myself to the class (even though everybody know me). I say my name is Precious Jones and this poem is for my baby son, Abdul Jamal Louis Jones. Then I let loose:

Mother to Son

Well, son, I'll tell you:
Life for me ain't been no crystal stair.

It's had tacks in it,
And splinters,
And boards torn up,
And places with no carpet on the floor—
Bare.
But all the time
I'se been a-climbin' on,
And reachin' landin's,
And turnin' corners,
And sometimes goin' in the dark
Where there ain't been no light.
So boy, don't you turn back.
Don't you set down on the steps
'Cause you finds it's kinder hard.
Don't you fall now—
For I'se still goin', honey,
I'se still climbin',
And life for me ain't been no crystal stair.

And after I finish everyone goin', Yeah! Yeah! Shoutin', Go Precious! And clapping and clapping and clapping. I felt very good.

Ms Rain say write our fantasy of ourselves. How we would be if life was perfect. I tell you one thing right now, I would be light skinned, thereby treated right and loved by boyz. Light even more important than being skinny; you see them light-skinned girls that's big an' fat, they got boyfriends. Boyz overlook a lot to be wif a white girl or yellow girl, especially if it's a boy that's dark skin wif big lips or nose, he will go APE over yellow girl. So that's my first fantasy, is get light. Then I get hair. Swing job, you know like I do with my extensions, but this time it be my own hair, permanently.

Then, this part is hard to say, because so much of my heart is love for Abdul. But I be a girl or woman—yeah girl, 'cause I would still be a girl now if I hadn't had no kids. I would be a virgin like Michael Jackson, like Madonna. I would be a different Precious Jones. My bress not be big, my bra be little 'n pink like fashion girl. My body be like Whitney. I would be thighs not big etc etc. I would be tight pussy girl no stretch marks and torn pussy from babies's head bust me open. That HURT. Hours hours push push push! Then he out, beautiful. Jus' a beautiful baby. But I'm not. I'm eighteen years old. One time boy come to Advancement House to see girlfriend, he think I'm somebody's mother. That bother me.

So there if I have a fantasy it be how I look. Ms Rain say I am beautiful like I am. Where? How? To who? To not have no kids mean I woulda had a different life. Counselor ask me one time is it the kids or is it I get raped to have 'em. Bofe; 'cause even if I not raped, who want a baby at twelve! Thas how old I was when I had Little Mongo.

What is a normal life? A life where you not 'shamed of your mother. Where your friends come over after school and watch TV and do homework. Where your mother is normal looking and don't hit you over the head wif iron skillet. I would wish for in my fantasy a second chance. Since my first chance go to Mama and Daddy.

Ms Rain always saying write remember write remember. Counselor say talk about it, talk about it— the PAST. What about *NOW*! At least wif school I am gettin' ready for my future (which to me is right now).

I don't know why I don't like counselor but Ms Rain say TALK, it gonna make things better whether I like her or not. But you know she jus' another social worker scratching on a pad. I know she writing reports on me. Reports go in file. File say what I could get, where I could go—if I could get cut off, kicked out Advancement House. Make me feel like Mama.

Me and Ms Weiss in counsel room. She as' me what's my earliest memory of Mama.

Huh?

"What's your earliest memory of your mother?"

Last week it was Daddy Daddy. She on a "Mama" kick this week. I don't say nuffin'.

"Precious?"

I can't move, speak. It's like second grade again, paralyzed. Tired of this honky askin' me questions. And I do need someone to talk, but not this hoe. But the room here is nice, you know, big sunshine window, dark green leather furniture, pictures on wall. I'm on big green couch. She behind desk in swivel chair. On the side of her is file cabinets.

"Can I get you anything?"

"Soda." I don't say water. I could go get that myself. She know I ain' got no money. Only way I'm gonna get soda is if she buy me one. Machine down in laundry room. Advancement House rules—staff do not give clients money (let's face it some of these bitches who act so s'perior 'n shit usta be crack addicts).

"What kind?"

"Cherry Coke."

Soon as she close door behind her I'm up. Moving fast quiet. But inside slow torture walk like I'm walking through glue. Nervous, I can smell my sweat stinking. If she was to walk in on me now I turn around and slap her cracker ass down. Problem not crack but the CRACKER! Farrakhan say. Big beige file cabinet behind her desk. A–J one drawer, K–Z on next drawer. Jones, Jones (it's a very common name); no P Jones, oh thas right, they late! Got me under Claireece Jones. Yup, here it is, JONES, CLAIREECE P. 'n underneef my name, social security number, 015-11-9153. I *fly* back to big green chair, stuff file in my backpack. I'm wiping sweat off my forehead when Ms Weiss walk back in room.

"It is hot in here, isn't it?" she say.

"Yeah," I say. She hand me soda. I say thank you.

"Anything come up while I was gone?"

Shake my head.

"You know you can use your notebook in between sessions—"

"I do."

"I mean you can use it specifically for something like this, trying to recover your first memory of your mother."

I already know what I'm gonna recover, the smell of Mama's pussy in my face.

"What're you thinking?"

"Nothing."

"Well let me know what comes up for you during the week. Write it in your notebook OK?"

"OK."

"You know your mother's been calling here wanting to come visit."

"No, I didn't know that."

"Would you like to have her come into a counseling session with you?"

"I don't know, I never think about it before."

"Well one more thing to think about before I see you next week."

Get up, grab my backpack. "Bye," I say. Go upstairs to pay phones outside nursery, call Rita, she not home yet, she probably at one of her meetings. Call Jermaine, she home, don't tell her what I done did, jus' say it's real important can she git over here. She say yes.

When she git here I pull file out backpack, don't know why I didn't want to read it alone. Don't know if it's because I'm afraid of what it will say or if I'm afraid I won't be able to read it, maybe both. I start reading.

"I have just finished a session with Claireece Precious Jones. Precious, as she likes to be called, (I guess so bitch it's my name!) is an eighteen-year-old African

PUSH

American female. According to her teachers at Each
One Teach One where she attends school she is a (I
don't know what that word is!) p-h-e-n-o-m-e-n-a-l
success." (Jermaine lean over my shoulder, say she not
sure about that one herself but judging from the con-
tents it must be good!) "Having made strides so tre—
men . . . tremendous! in the past year she was given the
mayor's award for outstanding achievement. She seems
to be actively en . . ." ("Engaged," Jermaine say) "in all
aspects of the learning process? However, (oh oh, when
white bitch start with *however*!) her TABE test scores
are disappointingly low." ("Not to Ms Rain! Not to Ms
Rain!" I say.) "She scored 2.8 on her last test." ("So
what! Ms Rain—" Jermaine interrupt, "Git a grip and
gon' read the report and don't get all emotional about
what this piece of shit white bitch got to say. Anyway, if
your shit wasn't dope you wouldn't be standin' up here
readin' what, what's her name?" "Ms Weiss." "What Ms
Weiss got to say.") "She will need at least an 8.0 before
she can enter G.E.D. class and begin work toward her
high school e-q . . . " ("Equivalency," Jermaine say. I
wanna say, I know, don't tell me the word 'less I ax! But
I never say anything like that to Jermaine.)

"Abdul is the client's (oh, now I'm *the client*) second
child; born in 1988, he's from all outwhere" (Jermaine
say, "That's 'outward' ") "OK, from all *outward* appear-
ances, a healthy and well adjusted toddler (he's a boy!).
Precious attends to his needs a-s-s-i-d-u-o-s-l-y (whatever!) and with great affection and ee-" ("Eagerly," Jer-

maine say) "seeks any and all information on child rear-
ing. (I guess so I'm his mother!) The client . . . " (I'm
the client again! I feel bullshit coming. I actually *feel*
sick. I hand the papers to Jermaine tell her, "Finish
reading.") "The client talks about her desire to get her
G.E.D. and go to college.

"The time and resources it would require for this
young woman to get a G.E.D. or into college would be
considerable. Although she is in school now, it is not a
job readiness program. Almost all instruction seems to
revolve around language a-c-" (Jermaine spelling now)
"q, a-kwi-si-tion acquisition!" ("What that?" I ask. "You
know, to get. Language acquisition, to get some language.") "The teacher, Ms Rain, places great emphasis
on writing and reading books. Little work is done with
computers or the variety of multiple choice pre-G.E.D.
and G.E.D. workbooks available at low cost to JPTA
programs.

"Precious is capable of going to work now. In January
of 1990 her son will be two years old. In keeping with the
new initiative on welfare reform I feel Precious would
benefit from any of the various workfare programs in
existence. Despite her obvious intellectual limitations
she is quite capable of working as a home attendant." ("A
home attendant? I don't wanna be no mutherfucking
home attendant! I wanna be—" "HUSH!" Jermaine say.)

"My rapport with Precious is minimal. Although I
am not sure with whom, she evidently has access to
counseling services provided by Each One Teach One.

She has a history of sexual abuse and is HIV positive."
("She say she not put that in my file! Bitch!" "If you told
it to her it's in there. That's that bitch's job, to get the
goods on you!" Jermaine say.) "The client seems to
view the social service system and its proponents as her
enemies, and yet while she mentions independent living, seems to envision social services, AFDC, as taking
care of her forever."

Jermaine hand me the file. "No way!" I scream. "I'm
getting my G.E.D., a job, and a place for me and Abdul,
then I go to college. I don't wanna 'home attend'
nobody."

"Be quiet!" Jermaine hiss. "And put this shit back
before you get in trouble!" I just sit there. She push the
file at me again. "Put this away. We'll talk about it with
Ms Rain in the morning."

"Let's put our chairs in a circle class," Ms Rain say, "and
do a little writing in our journals, then we'll talk. If you
want to focus on the topic introduced by Precious—"

"What topic?" Aisha, loud India girl from Guyana.

"Workfare and education."

"What about it?" Bunny, *real* skinny girl wif broke
teeth, say.

"Anything about it or nothing at all; if you want to
focus on the topic fine but you don't have to if you don't
want to. You have twenty minutes to write in your journal." She look at her watch, then say, "GO."

5/3/89

It's not like I in no big state of shock. I knew white bitch had something up her sleeve. Ms Weiss. Fuck her. I don't need her if all she see for me is wiping ol white people's ass. I ain been going threw all this learning to read and write so I be no mutherfucking home attendint. Rhonda usta hafta go all the way out to Brighton Beech wher she work for them mutherfuckers.

If I'm working twelve hours a day, sleeping in peoples houses like what Rhonda usta do, who will take care of Abdul? The ol white peoples had her there all day and night, "on call," they call it. But you only get pay for 8 hours (is the other 16 hours slavry?) so that's $8 \times \$3.35 = \$26.80$ dollars a day, but then you is not really getting that much cause you is working more than eight hours a day. You is working 24 hours a day and $\$26.80$ divided by 24 is $\$1.12$. Rhonda say ol bitch would ring a bell when she want Rhonda in the night. Home attendints usually work six days a week. I would only see Abdul on Sundays? When would I go to school? Why I gotta change white woman's diaper and then take money from that and go pay a baby sitter to change my baby's diaper? And what about school? How would I keep up with my reading and writing if I can't keep going to school?

I got to work it out before Abdul's birthday. Thas when the letters start coming. Letter say, you wish to keep receiving Aid to Families with Dependent Children report to XYZ place by such and such a date or your money will be cut. I mean I don't know exactly what it say but I got the drift, so many girls done told me what happen to them.

"OK," Ms Rain say. "Time is up for now, does anyone want to share?"

I'm only one raise my hand.

"OK Precious, go for it," she say.

"I don't really wanna read all I wrote, I jus' wanna kinda say what it is I'm writing about and how it came about. And how I'm really upset—"

"What *happened*?" Aisha say.

"Well to make a long story short the counselor at Advancement House pumping me about Mama and Daddy etc, etc, but it's really about workfare—"

"How you know?" Rhonda ax.

"'Cause I stole my file from Advancement House and read it. All this, 'What you wanna be?' and 'You can talk to me.' They ain' no mutherfucking therapists on our side they just flunkies for the 'fare."

Jermaine bust in. "If all they wanna do is place us in slave labor shits and we want to keep going to school, then that means they have a different agenda from us. I wanna work, but not for no mutherfucking welfare check in Central Park. And I be displacing brothers and sisters who really got jobs cleaning up 'cause I'm there working for free. And what kinda shit is it for someone like Precious to have to quit school before she get her G.E.D. to work at some live-in job for old crackers and shit. She'll never make a rise she get stuck in some shit like that!"

"Yeah," Ms Rain say, "but is stealing—"

"Ms Rain, I didn't steal that file I wouldn't know what my difficulties was!"

"You read the whole thing by yourself?" Ms Rain ask.

"Yeah, basically," I say, then, "Am I gonna hafta go be home attendant?"

"No!" Ms Rain say. "So stop worrying about it. We cross that bridge when we come to it. Trust me," she say, then, "No, trust *yourself*. But what I'm worried about right now is, if this Ms Weiss is someone they have you talking to to try to work out your history with and you can't trust her, you're not getting the help you need."

"Well, I just write in my notebook till I git wif some kinda therapist I can trust. Actually that help me more than talking to her. Plus I'm going to start going to meetings wif Rita for insect survivor—"

"*Incest*," girl name Bunny say.

"Thas what I mean."

"Well, it ain't what you been saying."

"So, what's the big deal insect, incest?" I say.

"One's where your parents molest you, the other is like a roach or bugs," Bunny say.

I crack up laffing.

Ms Rain look at me funny and say, "Precious have you ever had your hearing tested?"

"No," I say. I have never really had nothing tested. Glasses is what I really want so my eyes not get so tired at night when I be reading. But you can't get all hung up on details when you trying to survive.

"OK, let's put our chairs back in rows and get to work on our business letters we started last week."

For the past week or so Jermaine been putting her story in the book. Title, just the title done upset the class, *Harlem Butch*. What kinda title is that! Jermaine done wrote it like a poem. She bes' writer. We can't wait to read it.

I write everyday now, sometimes for an hour. Ms Rain, she call and say I am staying late for after school activities and babysitter keep Abdul till 2 p.m. and the following week I get extra money in my voucher for lunch (not that I can eat lunch *today* wif money from next week, but you know still . . .). I think about my future a lot. I think a lot. All the time. Ms Rain say I am intellectually alive and curious. I am just trying to figure out what is going on out here. How what happen to me could happen in modern days. I guess I am still trying to figure out just what *has* happen to me.

What has happen to me? I cannot just talk it to white social worker. She look at me like I am ugly freak did something to make my own life like it is. And she is trying to make me go to work wiping old white people's ass.

When I have a baby at twelve—

I don't want to cry. I tell myself I WILL NOT cry when I am writing, 'cause number one I stop writing and number two I just don't always want to be crying like white bitch on TV movies. Since I ain' no white bitch. I understand that now. I am not white bitch. I am not Janet Jackson or Madonna on the *inside*. I always thought I was someone different on the inside. That I was just fat and black and ugly to people on the OUT-SIDE. And if they could see *inside* me they would see something lovely and not keep laughing at me, throwing spitballs (shit one time nigger at school just spit on me when I was pregnant) and polly seed shells at me, that Mama and Daddy would recognize me as . . . as, I don't know, Precious! But I am not different on the inside. Inside I thought was so beautiful is a black girl too. But I am going to say what I was going to say. And then. I am going to put it all behind me and never say it again. I don't blame nobody. I just want to say when I was twelve, TWELVE, somebody hadda help me it not be like it is now. If—Ms Rain say "if" and "but" might be two of the most useless words in the language, at times that is, she say, 'cause if they was really useless they would disappear from use. Why no one put Carl in jail after I have baby by him when I am twelve? Is it my fault because I didn't talk to polices?

Tonight is the night Rita gonna take me down to Incest Survivor meeting. We going on bus. Harlem is small, but when you *in* it it look like the world. I have a subway map on my bedroom door, show all the places the subway go. Subway go to Queens, Brooklyn—I look at it sometimes and wonder where I be if I get on train and go to end of the line or get off at say, ummm, let's see, how about Lefferts Blvd in Queens or Middletown Road in the Bronx? What kinda town or part of New York it will be. Jermaine say be a white boy with a baseball bat when you get out of the subway. Rita say it's NOT true, or if it be true it's only part true.

So here I go! Precious going downtown. Precious what never go to summer camp; hear kids talk about going to camp where crackers is. Fresh Air funds and police league and shit. A land of tents and lakes. But maybe if I had gone to camp it be jus' like school in ol' days—no friends. Me 'n Rita get the 102 downtown. Rita done got her teef fixed. New guy she with got money. White guy. Got HIV too. He *loves* Rita. He was addict (I didn't know crackers was addicts). His parents stop giving him money when he was addict. But now he's sick they want to give him everything. Plus he got necktie job, briefcase, the whole bit. Rita got dream, he behind it. We all behind it. Rita want house in Harlem for HIV womens and their kids. I can get behind that. In my journal I write:

> bus wheel
> turn me
> through time
> past a Mama mama

first you see
the buildings like watching
a cartoon backwards
seem to be getting putted
back together
it's weird. (I am homer on a voyage
but from our red bricks in piles
of usta be buildings
and windows of black
broke glass eyes.
we come to buildings bad
but not *so* bad
street cleaner
then we come to a place
of
everything is fine
big glass windows
stores
white people
fur
blue jeans
its a different city
I'm in a different city
Who I be I grow up
here?
where a poodle dog
is not on tv
but walking down the street
on skinny white

> bitch lease.
> This whose ass
> they want
> me to wipe?
> Push wheelchair for—
> I kill 'em first.
>
> TYGER TYGER
> BURNING BRIGHT
>
> That's what in Precious
> Jones heart—a tyger.
> bookstores
> cafe
> BLoomydales!
> Bus keep on rolling

We git off at 14th Street. Rita say we can get cross-town bus or walk. I say walk; so we walk over to Seventh Avenue where Lesbian and Gay Center Building is. Rita not gay but this is where meeting is. We are going to Tuesday night Survivors of Incest Anonymous. I never been here before. Ms Rain, Rita, Rhonda, and Jermaine and house mom, all say GO. So I am good to go!

The center is big.

When I git in meeting I don't say nothing. It's people sitting in a circle. I'm spozed to talk. I will never talk here! To talk I have to tell how I feel in my body. The war. My body my head I can't say it right. How cum I'm so young and feel so old. So young like I don't know nuffin', so old like I know everything. A girl have her father's dick in her mouth know things the other girls don't know but it's not what you want to know.

It's all kinda girls here! They sitting in circle faces like clocks, no bombs. Bombs with hair and titties and dresses. After I sit here five minutes I know I am a bomb too. Only sitting here doing whatever they gonna do will keep me from blowing up. Thank you Rita for git me here on time.

"Hello." She look like a movie star! Slim, long hair, eyes like stars, red lips. "My name is Irene. I am an incest survivor."

My mouth fall open. Someone like that.

"It started when I was, oh, about four or five years old with him fondling me" (feeling her up). "By the time I was twelve he was having intercourse with me three or four times a week."

Everything is floating around me now. Like geeses from the lake. I see the wings beating beating hear geeses. It's more birds than geeses. Where so many birds come from. I see flying. Feel flying. *Am* flying. Far up, but my body down in circle. Precious is bird.

Someone is holding my hand. It's Rita. She is massage my hand. I come back from being a bird to hear beautiful girl crying. Smell Mama. Carl, the way his knees on either side of my neck.

Girl say, "Thank you for letting me share." She say, "This is a Tuesday night beginner's meeting. To share raise your hand." I raise my hand. My hand is going up through the smell of Mama, my hand is pushing Daddy's dick out my face.

"I was rape by my father. And beat." No one is talking except me. "Mama push my head down in her . . ." I can't talk no more. Beautiful girl whisper to me, "Are you through?" I say yes. She say, "Pick the next person." I look up from my shoes, Nikes; girls got they hand up. I pick girl in overalls with blue eyes. Grab Rita's hand, listen. Listen to girl rape by brother, listen to old woman rape by her father; don't remember till he die when she is 65 years old. Girls, old women, white women, lotta white women. Girl's younger sister murdered by the *cult*? Jewish girl, we had money on Long Island (like Westchester), my father was a prominent child psychiatrist. It started when I was about nine years old. Girls like Jermaine is, I am a proud lesbian. But it's the only thing I'm proud of; I was confine to a mental institution for fourteen years, diagnosed as a schizophrenia—

What am I hearing!

One hour and a half women talk. Can this be done happen to so many people? I know I am not lying! But is they? I thought cult was in movie. What kinda world this babies raped. A father break a girl's arm. Sweet talk you suck his dick. All kinda women here. Princess girls, some fat girls, old women, young women. One thing we got in common, no *the* thing, is we was rape.

Afterwards we go out for coffee. I have never been "out for coffee" before. Rita put her arm around my shoulder, I order hot chocolate 'cause that's what I like. Blond girl who is airline stewardess say, "Precious! That's a beautiful name!"

I'm alive inside. A bird is my heart. Mama and Daddy is not win. I'm winning. I'm drinking hot chocolate in the Village wif girls—all kind who love me. How that is so I don't know. How Mama and Daddy know me six- teen years and hate me, how a stranger meet me and love me. Must be what they already had in they pocket.

It's a black girl across the table from me with long pretty hair in dreadlocks like Ms Rain. But not wild like Ms Rain. I surprise myself. "How you get your hair like that?" I say.

"Oh," she say, "you like it? I do yours one day you want. That's what I do—fix people's hair and makeup." She give me a card!

Rita ask me do I want another hot chocolate. I do but don't want to be greedy. Even if boyfriend do give her money she got better things to spend it on then Precious Jones. She hug me and ask waitress, "Could I have another hot chocolate and cappuccino." I like how Rita is, she know the world, how to act and stuff. Some- times I don't have a clue!

Well, today counseling session wif Mama. She call here, call here, *call* here, asking social worker to see me. I tell Ms Weiss no. Then Ms Weiss tell me I *should* see her. Why I should? I ask. For your own good, for yourself, to see what she has to say. Spozed to meet today 4 p.m.

Watch say one minute to four. Down one two three four five six seven eight steps, then a little landing then eight more steps. I walk through door, one minute past four. What she want now?

Mama sitting on big green couch. Ms Weiss looking at me waiting for me to sit down. I sit down. Ms Weiss say to Mama, "Well Mrs Johnston, may I call you Mary?"

"I don't care." Mama look down at her shoes which is big men's loafers. Room smell all funny. Mama stink. Got on big orange-color sleeveless dress, torn under the arms. Hair fucked up. Eyes look stupid wifout red evil light on to hit you.

I think Ms Weiss jus' freak mind. Lie to Mama, bull-corn me. Probably Mama think coming here talking to Ms Weiss in counselin' session gonna git me back, me 'n Abdul. So why do that? I don't git what Ms Weiss doin'. I need house for me 'n Abdul. Advancement House is for womens and girls with newborn and young babies. I gotta be out of this mutherfucker soon. I wanna finish at Each One Teach One 'n gone get my G.E.D. I want maybe git Lil Mongo out retard house where she lay on floor in pee clothes but Ms Weiss wanna know my earliest memory of Mama? I open my notebook and look in it.

whut is my erliest ~~memry~~ memory of my mother?
a room that's small fillt up wif my parents. it
smell. can of mackerel left open in kitchen on hot

day that's what make me remember. that smell. he
put his ball in my face. years like wash machine
aroun and around. mama jaw open like evil wolf.
the smell deeper than toilet. her fingers pick
apart my pussy. night. poisoned rat. don't have
dreams.

I close my book.

"Well Mary, you want to begin by talking a little bit
about the abuse?" Ms Weiss say to Mama.

"What 'buse?"

"Well according to Precious' files she has had two
children by your boyfriend, the late Carl Kenwood Jones,
who is also *her father*? You've been calling here saying you
want to be reunited with your daughter and grandson,
that you want them to come home. Well I think you'd
better explain just what happened in that home."

Oh Mama, please don't go for this!

"Well, I, Precious, b'long at home."

Mama please be quiet.

"When did the abuse happen, how often, where?
When were you first aware of what was going on Ms
Johnston?"

"I guess, he come over you know. I wake up at night,
morning he not wif me, I know he in there wif her.
When it first start? I don' know. I'm a good mother. She
had everything. I done tole her that. Pink 'n white baby

carriage, little pink bootie socks, dresses; everything I put on her pink. Precious, she, so smiling and healthy. A day don't go by I don't take her out wheeling in the air. Even when it's cold I take her out, to church, to some-where, me 'n Carl—my husband, I call him—loves Pre-cious. I loves him. I dream of day we gonna you know, git married, git house wif grass, color TVs in all the rooms. Precious she born about the same time as Miz West son that got kilt. You remember him don't you Precious?"

What is she talkin' about!

"He born summertime 'bout same time as you."

"I born November," I say. Least that what I always thought.

"Yeah yeah thas right. My little Scorpio chile! Scor-pio's crafty. I ain' sayin' they lie, jus' you cain't always trust 'em. But anyway Precious 'bout the same age as Gary, Miz West son got kilt, give or take a few months! But ooh wheee! Precious fast! She walkin' talkin'—everything 'fore Miz West son. Her teef, everything. Teef growing like Bugs Bunny or something! She can do little dance steps and he hardly walking. I put on Kool and the Gang, remember Precious, you remem-ber? I put on Kool and the Gang and you disco to that? She had a happy childhood all 'n all, Carl jus' a high-natured man . . ."

I don't believe Mama! Why don't she jus' shut up with this diarrhea shit!

"When? I don't know when it start. When I remember it? She still little. Yeah, around three maybe. I give her a bottle. I still got milk in my bresses but not for her but from Carl sucking. I give him tittie, Precious bottle. Hygiene, you know?"

"Huh?" Ms Weiss go.

"Huh?" go Mama back.

"You mentioned something about hygiene in connection with . . . with . . . " Ms Weiss can't finish.

"I bottle her, tittie him. Bottle more better for kidz. Sanitary. But I never git dried up 'cause Carl always on me. It's like that you know. Chile, man—a woman got bofe. What you gonna do? So we in bed. I put her on one side of me on pillow, Carl on other side me."

Ms Weiss look like she done stopped breathing.

"Carl got my tittie in his mouf. Nuffin' wrong wif that, it's natural. But I think thas the day IT start. I don't never remember nothing before that. I hot. He sucking my tittie. My eyes closed. I know he getting hard I can see wifout my eyes, I love him so much."

Umm hmm, I was raised by a psycho maniac fool.

"He climb on me, you know. You unnerstand?"

No, tell us some more stupid bitch.

"So he on me. Then he reach over to Precious! Start wif his finger between her legs. I say Carl what you doing! He say shut your big ass up! This is good for her. Then he git off me, take off her Pampers and try to stick his thing in Precious. You know what trip me out is it almost can go in Precious! I think she some kinda freak baby then. I say stop Carl stop! I want him on *me*! I never wanted him to hurt her. I didn't want him doing *anything* to her. I wanted my man for myself. Sex me up, not my chile. So you cain't blame all that shit happen to Precious on *me*. I love Carl, I love him. He her daddy, but he was my man!"

Ms Weiss look at me now. "Precious, you've been writing in your journal about this."

"This and other stuff."

"She write poems too, lady at Each One Teach One say." This from Mama. Mama one hundred, not ninety nine, percent crazy.

"Would you like to share some of that in this session?" Ms Weiss ask.

"No."

"Why not?"

"Ms Rain say journal completely confidential. Share if you want. If you don't want to, don't. I don't want to."

I'm gone. It's 4:45 p.m. Up! One, two, three, four, five, six, seven, eight steps. I hate Mama, she ain' shit. I feel like nothing around her, like *minus* nothing. I gotta get outta here.

I go down to kitchen where house mother is. "Miz Mom!"

"Stop screaming!" she say. "What's wrong with you?"

"You could get Abdul from nursery, feed him, and

keep a eye on him till I get back so I could go to Body Positive meeting?"

"Tonight's not your night—"

"Pleeezzze I gotta get outta here!"

"What happened with your mama?"

"'You cain't blame all what happened to Precious on *me*. I wanted *my man* for *myself!*'" I imitate Mama.

"I wanted my man for myself! Now ain' that one to go down in the history books. Yeah, I'll keep that little ol' bad boy! You got a lot of time before six-thirty, why don't you git you some dinner before you run out of here?"

"I was gonna take my journal book and write on the bus, 'steadda taking the train."

She go in her pocket get out that ol' blue change purse, so ol' it look like somebody blue grandmother and hand me three dollars. Something tear inside me. I wanna cry but I can't. It's like something inside me keeps ripping but I can't cry. I think how *alive* I am, every part of me that is cells, proteens, nutrons, hairs, pussy, eyeballs, nervus sistem, brain. I got poems, a son, friends. I want to live so bad. Mama remind me I might not. I got this virus in my body like cloud over sun. Don't know when, don't know how, maybe hold it back a long long time, but one day it's gonna rain.

I start to cry but it's 'cuz I'm mad. Miz Mom wipe my face give me two more dollars!

"Umm, I should cry more often!"

"Ain' you about a mess! Git outta here!"

I git my jacket 'n my shades. Everybody in this house

go to meetings, in "recovery." What I'm in recovery for? I ain' no crack addict. I git so mad sometimes. Mama jus' pour my life down the drain like it's nothing. I got all this shit to deal wif.

"Don't forget your notebook," Miz Mom.

Everybody know I write poems. People respect me. I get outside. It's raining. Good.

The meeting is good, it's for HIV positive girls 16–21. Ms Rain say people who help you most (*sometimes*) is ones in the same boat. I started putting my story in the big book at school. I want to get it done before I graduate out to G.E.D.

Last week we went to the museum. A whole whale is hanging from the ceiling. Bigger than big! OK, have you ever seen a Volkswagen car that's like a bug? Um huh, you know what I'm talking about. That's how big the heart of a blue whale is. I know it's not possible, but if that heart was in me could I love more? Ms Rain, Rita, Abdul?

I would like to.

Abdul get tested. He is not HIV positive. Something like that make me feel what Rhonda, what Farrakhan, say—there is a god. But me when I think of it I'm more inclined to go wid Shug in *The Color Purple*. God ain' white, he ain' no Jew or Muslim, maybe he ain' even black, maybe he ain' even a "he." Even now I go downtown and seen the rich shit they got, I see what we got too. I see those men in vacant lot share one hot dog and they homeless, that's good as Jesus with his fish. I remember when I had my daughter, nurse nice to me—all that is god. Shug in *Color Purple* say it's the "wonder" of purple flowers. I feel that, even though I never seen or had no flowers like what she talk about.

I'm not happy to be HIV positive. I don't understand why some kids git a good school and mother and father and some don't. But Rita say forgit the WHY ME shit and git on to what's next.

I don't know what's next. I took the TABE test again, this time it's 7.8. Ms Rain say quantum leap! Like I was one place and instead of step up, it's a leap! What does that score actually mean? I read according to the test around 7th or 8th grade level now. Before on test I score 2.0 then 2.8. The 2.0 days was really low days because I could not read at all (test just give you 2.0 even if you don't fill in nothing). I got to get up to the level of high school kids, then college kids. I know I can do this. Ms Rain tell me don't worry it's gonna work out. I still got time.

It's Sunday, no school, meetings. I'm in dayroom at Advancement House, sitting on a big leather stool holdin' Abdul. The sun is coming through the window splashing down on him, on the pages of his book. It's called *The Black BC's*. I love to hold him on my lap, open up the world to him. When the sun shine on him like this, he is an angel child. Brown sunshine. And my heart fill. Hurt. One year? Five? Ten years? Maybe more if I take care of myself. Maybe a cure. Who knows, who is working on shit like that? Look his nose is so shiny, his eyes shiny. He my shiny brown boy. In his beauty I see my own. He pulling on my earring, want me to stop daydreaming and read him a story before nap time. I do.

<u>LIFE STORIES</u>

Our Class Book

Reading 1   MWF 9-12 a.m.

Higher Education Alternative /
Each One Teach One

Blue Rain, Instructor

everi mornin
by Precious j.

Everi mornin
i write
a poem
before I go to
school
marY Had a little lamb
but I got a kid
an HIV
that folow me
to school
one day.

mornin
by Precious Jones

Mornin is a rooteen
up at 6 a.m.
wash teef, dress
      wash Abdul teef, face, booty
      dress him
Breakfast for kids
      we go to kitchen
      fix him something
      good from what's there
      what's there for baby
      is good
oatmeal
cream wheat
rice cream
appul sauc
      or egg toast
      bacon   I don't let Abdul eat bacon
Put Abdul wif a kiss
      in nother woman arms

```
rootine b
         r
          e
          a k
i run get dress
     fix tea (don't like coffee)
     grab books
             walk
     mornin wet the streets
     amung the vakent trees
          is secrit plots
          of green diamonds
          call grass.
```

MY LIFE
by Rita Romero

Our house, which was an apartment, was full of beautiful stuff—velvet couch, lace curtain, virgin statues, candles, and chandeliers. My mother was like a medium. Not santeria—throw shells, yellow flowers for Oshun and all that but more the gypsy trip—cards and crystal ball. Always people in and out our house; nice people, give me a caramel or sourball, pat on the head. My mother was dark, moreno? Like we got 1 million words for color, Puerto Ricans. But to me, everyone, she was beautiful. She look like, you ever seen that movie star from way back, Dorothy Dandridge—that's what Mami look like, only Mami's hair is like a black river, thick long down her back. Eyes, I always think Mami's eyes is olives. Black things that could see but so rich you could eat. Maybe, I giggle, if you could eat Mami's eyes you could see in the crystal ball too.

My father honestly I don't remember
him so much even though I know he was
there everyday. I know he is white
because he tells me this, tells me I am
white. I wanna be what Mami is, not what
he is. Mami says he is just another
brainwashed spic. He had a shop on
Tremont Ave where he work on wreck cars.
From Mami is beans and rice, roast pork,
flan, the pink and yellow lace dresses
I wear to Mass. From him is be quiet be
quiet go help your mother clean this
place up it's a mess it's a mess speak
English speak English SPEAK ENGLISH.
It's because of him I don't speak Spanish. He tell Mami talk English talk
English make the kids speak English.
You want 'em to grow up like you puta
can't get a job. Puta, whore bitch I
know what you're doing with these guys
while I'm out working my ass off. I ever
catch I kill you whore, hear me I kill
you. Then he grab me, hold out my arm
next to his, see SEE. Look he says you
are WHITE. You are not no nigger morena
puta WHORE. He's crazy he don't make
sense. Mami is not that. He scream at

Mami, "My kids are WHITE!" Mami just look scared.

I'm six years old. The walls of the room are maroon. The velvet couch with the white lace doilies is the same color as the wall. It is so pretty. It's my favorite. In the middle is the dark wood table with the crystal ball. Lace curtains is on the window. The shades is drawn. What's inside is prettier, outside is just a brick wall. The table has a glass top on it. The edges of the glass where it's cut is green colored, I like that. The crystal ball is big. Mami is at the table, her hair is black down her back, her lips like red movie star lips, eyes black like oil, looking at me. She hands me a sourball, it's my favorite; it's melting in my mouth. By the time it melts I know she be going shoo shoo Negra, I got someone coming. Meaning one of the worry face clients talking in Spanish about somebody dead, in jail or in the arms of another, would be there.

But the taste of the sour ball stays on my tongue forever. It's Papi walk through the door. He don't say Mamita, he say Bitch! You think I'm crazy. I KNOW que tu puede. I KNOW PUTA! And he pull gun from his pants, shoot Mami—bang bang bang. Her brains fly out her head her mouth open blood blood blood everywhere, it look like one olive is hanging out her head like a man off a cliff. She never speak nothing, fall out chair, go gurgle sound, more blood fall out her mouth. Her dress, hair, the carpet is red. Papi standing there, start crying.

If I close my eyes I could see Puerto Rico—someplace water is blue jewels, palm trees, mangoes, music like Willie Colon all the time. But I never been there. Would it be different if I had been born there steadda here? He kill her there steadda here? What's the difference? Go back? To where you never been? I'm better off here with the AIDS thing and stuff. The health care ain't shit here for addicts but it's better than P.R. my brother say. He went to P.R. die. I got friends here and stuff.

Ms Rain, senora La Lluvia, ask me to write more, write about my life now. Just talk some more in the tape recorder and she transcribe it. What life? Foster care, rape, drugs, prostitution, HIV, jail, rehab. Everybody like to hear that story. Tell us more tell us more more MORE about being a dope addict and a whore! Puta tecata puta tecata. But I tell you what *I* want, it's *my* book—we had a nice place, velvet things, lace curtains, the crystal ball. I ask her once my hand in the black river of her hair, my eyes looking up at hers, her caramel color skin, red movie lips, the perfume from her like a pink and purple dream—show me Mami how to see. Show me what's inside the crystal ball. She look at it a long time then say, Ahh Negrita, you don't want to know.

MY YOUNGER YEARS
by Rhonda Patrice Johnson

My younger years was actually spend
in Jamaica which is where my family is
from. It was me my brother and my mother
and father who we call Ma and Pop.
Things was good there until Pop die then
we didn't have money so we move to the
U.S. For me that is when the problem
start. What the problem is is hard to
say but it was with my brother.

My mother git a restaurant on 7th
Ave. between 132nd and 133rd selling
West Indian take out. I work in the
restaurant from git up in the morning to
go to bed at night. I don't go to school
even. I could read and write some but
when we got here I was twelve already
and hadn't been going to school for a
long time in Jamaica. So my mother say,
you almost grown so what's the use. But
Kimberton, he's my brother go to
school. A lot go for Kimberton—clothes,
bicycle, computer toy. He is one year

younger than me. I wash down the
kitchen, scrub pots, pans, grill, all
that! Go to the big market with Ma at
Hunt's Point. Go to La Marqueta on Lex-
ington with Ma. I make peas and rice,
roti, cod fish cakes, goat curry, all
that! The people that want eat in we got
two little tables in the front near the
window. I serve people.

I fourteen when Kimberton start leaning on me. I don't know how else to tell
it.

"Ma, Kimberton leaning on me."

"What you telling?"

"He bothering me."

"Leave his computer stuff alone and
he will leave your dolls alone."

That's what he used to do in Jamaica,
break my dolly's head or arm off. I mean
something different now. He is the same
size as me. I try to fight him. We sleep
in same room. He wait until I am sleep.
I awake Kimberton standing over me on
top the bed naked as the day he born.
Thing like a donkey's. I don't want it.
My skin get bad. I don't know if it's

from that. I get a lot of pounds on me.
I'm always a quiet girl, I don't say
NOTHING now unless some one speak me.

I tell her again when I am 16. Kimberton is fifteen but he skipped a grade
in elementary school so he is in his
second year of high school. Going to be
a doctor. "You going to be a doctor!" my
mother tell him, "What you think I'm
working for, for you to be a god damn
taxi driver!" the question I ask myself
is, what am I working for.

"Ma."

"What!"

"Kimberton is . . . is molesting with
me at night." I don't know how to say
it. I can't say rape, that's not what
brothers do to sisters.

"Molesting with you? What kinda talk
is that?"

"You know—"

"No, I don't know! Miss Fresh."

"He come over my side of the room at
night and intercourse me."

She get quiet quiet. I smell the
curry goat stewing, peas 'n rice. I can

see through the glass door of refrigerator bottles of ginger beer, 7UP, Cokes
and maubey lined.

"Tell me what you talking about."

I tell her.

She say get out my house now. I say
but Ma! Leave now she start screaming
'bout what I done to her son. Filthy
haint, night devil walker she call me.
I am shocked. I think I am still in that
shock sometimes.

But it's like that sometime you know.
I done found out over the years you just
can't guess how people is gonna react.
You think common sense would make her
come out on my side. You know, mother
daughter, but it didn't happen that
way. She was screaming 'bout how I was
the oldest coulda shoulda stopped him.
what I believe is she think Kimberton
gonna be big doctor one day and retire
her from working twenty-four seven. An'
if someone got to go it not gonna be
him.

part two

MY GROWN UP YEARS

I'm twenty-four years old it's been eight years since I "left" (I put it like that cause you know how I left) my mother's house. Kimberton, he is dentist. Was a dentist, maybe he is, maybe he beat the case—he get charged by young girl's parents of trying to stick his finger (and who knows what else) up her pussy while he spozed to be fixing teeth! Far out huh? Ma tell me this. I don't go visit but I see her out on street when she doing her shopping. We talk like I'm her daughter that got married and move out or go away to nurse school or some such. I don't know, I just go along with the program. Ma say it's all lies, girl's parents just trying to extort him. But what I think is he pull his shit on the wrong one. You can't get away with everything all the time with everybody.

The first couple of years on the street was the worst. From working

under Ma, even though I do everything,
I really did not know how to get a job,
talk to social service—what's that! So
I was just out there! I would go with
men to bars, drink, go home with them,
hope I get to stay the night—that they
don't tell me go after they come. After
I do this with, oh, is it five or fifty
or a hundred guys, I start dissolve. I
don't know how else to explain it. I'm
strong woman, if you was looking at me
you could see this. Redbone, what Americans say, some color to her, Jamaicans
would say. Five foot eight inches,
heavy set, or fat some people would say.
Kimberton (who is dark) say I look like
a mutant, what ever that is. But after
the I don't know how many mens I start
to break into little pieces and the men
look funny, like worms is growing out of
their skins, worms that turn to little
penises, till I am sick with the walking dicks of Harlem. Everywhere is a
hand rubbing, a dick going psst psst
come here come here.

    I can't stay in shelters. I just
can't, they is crazy people houses. So

I just wander the street, get little money here and there. I meet this one guy, give me enough to get a room at the Y for one week, tell me to go down to welfare. I check that out. They are so nasty to me, send me so many different places to get so many different papers, things I don't have no way of getting! I don't have no birth certificate unless my mother got it but I know where I was born—Kingston, Jamaica. September 22, 1963. I say fuck the whole welfare thing. It's crazy. I walk out office but not before I break one white woman's nose. She send me to get a social security card. I tell her the number but she say got to have the card, go get a duplicate at downtown office. By the time I get back from downtown, where they tell me was an office I could go to on 125th Street, she got coat on talking 'bout she through for the day, going home. You know just as breezy as she can be! Come back tomorrow and she help me right off. What she saying, and she know it, spend another night in nowhere sleeping next to death. Git on that park bench, subway, rooftop—freeze, get stabbed, raped; I'm going home. I haul off and hit that bitch so hard whole room could hear her nose go CRUNCH.

At the Y this woman from Trinidad tell me about ol' white bitch in Brighton Beach she taking care of but she gonna hafta quit cause she got something better on Upper West Side wheeling some doctor's children to the park. Say she recommend me, don't need no social security card and all that.

So I work for ol' white woman with degenerative disease and mind to equal. HATE black people, always a "you people this" and "you people that." Call me to her daughter Swortkraus! "Swortkraus is a little slow today," what kinda goddam shit is that. But you know she ol' and helpless I forgive a lot. I think I could put a pillow over her face and no one know, no one care. But I would know, plus I be out of a job. I leave when she throw, try to, throw bed pan at me (end up spilling it on her self) cause she grandson, who she putting through NYU

medical school did not come to see her
when he say he would. She good and crazy.

I go back to welfare, this time I say
to myself, some money or jail. All the
Porta Ricans and American niggers can
get something—white people is getting
it too. Why can't I?

The security guards get me while my
thumbs is closing down on this white
devil's throat. Tell me cool down mama!
I'm not your mama! Everything is red, I
go end this cracker's days! They pull me
off, take four of 'em. I don't go to
jail though. They get me job! One of the
black guys, not even a desk to himself,
hand me a three by five card with a name
and address on it, tell me, go there. I
get position looking after ol' white
man, tubes all in him. He not so bad,
but he nasty. Want me to wash his penis
and carry on. On all the walls, I mean
on every wall, is a picture, I mean a
big picture of Michael Jordan. OK, 16
walls, you got it, 16 pictures of
Michael Jordan.

But he pay me. I get room with bathroom, things looking up for awhile, you

know. Then the ol' mutherfucker die.
After a while it's pretty hard again. I
get three day notice to pay or quit my
room. What I'm gonna do? I'm a person
don't just like to sit there. Just sit
there I be throw out for sure. I get
couple of big big garbage bags and start
going from trash can to trash can col-
lecting aluminum cans. To fill the bags
take awhile cause is some competition
out on the Harlem streets for these bottles and cans. But I am strong and desperate. I'm looking like a beetle bug or
something, hunched over with two huge
black garbage bags on my back. I'm on
Adam Clayton Powell Blvd which I usually avoid cause it's where Ma's
restaurant, ROTI 'N MORE Take Out or Eat
In, is. But today I don't care, I don't
wanna be homeless again. It happen
again I might not get up from it. I
gotta do something.

So I'm on the Avenue (which is also
the Boulevard) near 134th Street moving, trash can by trash can, toward
133rd. I pass ROTI 'N MORE. I look up

and see a FOR RENT sign in the window,
and next to sign is Kimberton. Our eyes
meet. His is shock, mine is like a kiss,
my brother! Always my first thought of
him is before he rape me then the memory roll in like fog. I see Kimberton's
mouth fall open at the horror of me bent
over, hands gripped around the black
bags. I remember my hands grating
coconut, washing rice, stirring peas,
scrubbing pots in cold greasy water,
pulling the catheter out the old man's
penis, scraping shit from old Mrs
Feld's age spot ass. I look back at him.
I am not ashamed. I could be dead all
these years. Rage hot fill me. Kimberton's eyes glowing like radioactive in
my mind, his fly eyes, his hands pushing me down on the bed, years. Years.
Kimberton comes to the door. He has on
some clothes that cost a lot and should
look great but he just look foreign and
skinny and dark. He don't look like
American man like he want to. I stare.
This a man fuck his sister and say so
what. This a man go to dental school,

graduate high school at sixteen. A credit to his family and race, Ma say. But I'm his family and race ain't I?

"What do you want?" he say.

I don't speak.

"Ma already buried. No one can find you to tell you."

Ma dead? The fog coming down on me. Kimberton step toward me, pull one hundred dollar bill from his wallet. To take it I would have to put the bags down. I look down at Kimberton's orange colored leather shoes, stupid pointed toes, and up to his head which is beginning to bald.

I figure I better get moving 'fore the fog is too thick to see my way out. Kimberton is walking behind me now saying stupid things. "We wondered about you." It's like some kinda dribble, his voice, that fall on top the fog. "You wanted it as much as I did!" he say. How could he say that. I keep walking, such a long way I have to go.

It's a guy at the soup kitchen, Asian guy, advocate from Young and Homeless, find out I got a work history get me job

cleaning office building over in East
Harlem. I get me a room over on Convent
Avenue from old light-skinned dude got
one of those big old prewar apartments,
renting out rooms. Tell me when his
mother had the place she rent room to
Marcus Garvey. My question is, did Marcus Garvey get heat? It's at rooming
place I meet Rita Romero, who is in
class, who tell me about school which is
how I get in this book.

   the end, no the BEGINNING

HARLEM BUTCH
by Jermaine Hicks

Why you wanna be a man?
Why you wanna be a man
man
man
why you wanna be
a man?
why you wanna be
a man
man
man?

Look it never occurred to me to dress
like a man! For Chrissake, what the fuck
is that? I was dressing like myself.
Myself.
I'm 7:
"Hurry up! Get dressed or you'll be
late for school!" my mother is shouting. The whole block can hear her for
sure. She has a mouth like an express
train. She has to be out the door by
eight to make sure she's not late for

the white woman she works for. My father
is already gone by 6 a.m. Every morning. I look down from the top of the
bunk beds to my brother's empty unmade
bed. The sheet is a gray tangle twist-
ing out underneath dingy blue poly
blankets. His brown corduroy pants are
red flags signalling something in my
7 year old soul. I jump out the top
bunk, pick up the pants and put them on.
That was seventeen years ago. They were
not my pants but I felt they should be.
I, how to describe a feeling so deep
it's like a river? How can a river be
wrong?
    "Take off those pants!"
    "No!"
    "Those are your brother's pants."
    "Git me some."
    "They're not lady like."
    "So what!"
    "It's wrong!"
    "Why?"
How can a river be wrong
a river that engorges my clitoris
and fills me?

. . .

Ms Rain, rivers, what makes rivers
run?
"Huh?"
A river, what makes it go, run?
"Well, I don't really know. I never
studied rivers in college. I mean, I
imagine some type of gravity, the
riverbed's resistance to absorption;
you know rainfall,
water running down hill—"
A river ever run wrong?
"What?"
Run wrong, a river ever run wrong?
"Well, they overflow—flood—"
she flailed.
Yes, that was the word, flailed,
flailed helplessly Ms. Rain did.
"In 1811, the Mississippi flowed
backwards due to an earthquake."
If I didn't have a record I'd join
the Navy,
Be ON water, IN water all the time!
(I could have passed my G.E.D. test
months, no a year ago. Ms Rain is
upset I won't take it. Taking it

will mean I will have to leave the
class.)
I'm still 7:
a boy holds me down
under the stairwell
that smells like urine
(pee I woulda said at seven)
tries to push his dick
into me.
I am 8:
when I put my tongue
in Mary-Mae's mouth
for the first time
(under the same steps)
9:
my fingers
10:
my tongue but this time
I put it in her
where he tried to put
it in me
13:
I am pressed close to her
against the wall
in her room
we will fall on the
still pink in some places

chenille bedspread
My fingers A trains howling thru her
dark tunnel
We will—
DADDY! DADDY!
Come LOOK what Mary-Mae and Jermaine
is doing!
BULLDAGGERBULLDAGGERBULLDYKE
DYKEBULLDYKEBULLDYKEDYKEDYKE
the voices become like the programmed messages in the subway time
unpredictable loud irritating
expected
but it is Mary-Mae's father who
catches me one night to show me
what a MAN is, what a woman is
when I get up from my new knowledge
one of my front teeth is gone
The doctor will tell my mother
damage is done
I won't tell her by who

I never told that part of my story
before because I hate to see their
square eyes light up with, "Oh that's
why! I understand now! I see—"

No! You don't see! Before I was
snatched out the air like a butterfly,
wings torn off me. BEFORE any all that
I had slid my fingers up the sweet stink
of another child and knelt down to lick
her thighs. Men did not make me this
way. Nothing happened to make me this
way. I was born butch!

I was 14:

my mother is a religious movement. I
don't know how else to describe it, a
walking church. A wake up, go to sleep,
jack off, shouting ass Christian. It
make me sick. JESUS this, JESUS that,
fuck that shit.

We are nuclear but poor

four of us

mother father sister brother sitting
around the white formica covered table,
little flecks of gold embedded like sunshine in the white plastic. We are eating breakfast, which is sardines out a
can emptied onto our plates and some
cold biscuits left over from last night.
He went to take a sip of coffee and she

said, "According to Luke Chapter 9, verse 16, Jezus took the five loaves and the two fishes and looking up at heaven—" And his arm flew out like a jack-in-the-box and snatched the Bible from her and threw it in her face HARD. Hitting her in the eye. A blood red spot grew and spread across her eye for seven days. By the time she went to Emergency she was another colored woman shoulda come in sooner story there's not really much we can do for you now except call in the medical students from NYU to stare at how stupid you people are and you can learn to see almost as well with one eye as you can with two.

So my mother—one eye, no man, two children and the Bible.

What hurt more than the dark hole of Daddy's leaving, than Mary-Mae's father raping me, more than seeing the spot grow in Mama's eye like a radioactive tomato, was seeing her afterward on the D train, holding her Bible over her head screeching, "HELL! You are going to hell! Unless you accept the word of God's only son JEEZUSS!! JEEEEEZZUUSSS!!! The train hurtling through the dark tunnel, the laughing pitying and annoyed eyes of the riders and my mother, blind eye, a snot colored marble in her chocolate face screaming, "JEZUS! JJEEEEEE-ZZZZUUUUUUSSSS!!!!!"

I'm 17:

when she walks in on me and Mary-Mae fucking. Can't she see we're in love?

No, she can't.

She starts to foam at the mouth screaming curses in the name of God. FILTHYSICKHELPMEJEZUSIDIDNTRAISEYOU-THISWAYFILTHYFILTHY The words float over our naked bodies like clouds of poison gas. They drop on us soiling Mary-Mae's long copper legs, smooth child free body. The smell of us sweet, stinky, swollen with sex contracts and dies in the air.

I love Mary-Mae.

I pull my underpants, jeans, shirt, shoes on, all in one seemingly impossible move. Mary-Mae is in a daze. The poison gas shaming her causing her to stumble. We fall out the room together and then the front door of the apartment. Mary-Mae turns down the hall to her father's apartment. I keep going until I hit the street. I never see Mary-Mae again.

I'm seventeen and parent free. An emancipated minor. I mean my father was not hard to find. In a tiny studio in Queens, where, "I'm welcome to stay as long as I want." But at night when he flops down on the convertible sofa, the kind you see advertised on the subway for five hundred dollars, I am left on a thin mat near the door listening to him masturbate. Does he think I'm asleep? In the morning over a breakfast of boiled eggs and salmon cakes that reminds me of sardines, he asks me if the floor isn't hard. The sardines remind me how swift and long his arms are. The sun coming through his window is a blood red spot that covers the sky.

So I step out on the street that morning, on my own, like Huck Finn or some shit, it's been like that ever since—Harlem, The Village, The Bronx, Queens—I know my way around. I bartend, drive

cab, do maintenance. I was super over on
126th and Madison for three years. But
I want more than pushing a mutherfucking broom, or slooshing fire juice to
other broom pushers. So I came back to
school. I knew from day one I should be
in G.E.D. class but I know I never
woulda wrote this story with those
dickheads in there. I never would have
stayed.

My face? My eye, ear? Ms Rain say you
might want to write about that? Write
about six grown men,

I'm 19: by then. What can I say except
I fought back. And when it's six men
that means you put your fist up and try
to hit at least one of 'em 'fore they
kill you. I'm with Rita, on that some
things don't need to be written about.
For example, how it sounds when a fist
with two hundred pounds behind it con-
nects solidly with your eye. Or the way
concrete does not yield to lip cheek
nostril when they meet. And a razor, the
closest thing it feels like is extreme
cold. Cold so cold it's hot, a laser
separating.

I woke up in Harlem Hospital. Like Mama one eye messed up ear too. But the Bible did not save me. I saved myself. Am still saving myself. That was the second time men took me to school. Only time I don't have a gun on me now is when I go to sleep, even then, Mary-Mae, as I call my rod, is not far away.

It's not over yet!

Jermaine

untitled
by Precious Jones

Rain, wheels, bus
car,
only in dreams
I have car
me n Abdul riding like
in the movies
sun a yellow red ball
rising over hills
where indeins usta live
beaches, Islands
where Jamaica-talks live
Bob Marley
song
first I don't unnerstan it
but now I do
CONCREET JUNGLE
it's a prison days
we live in
at least me
I'm not really free
baby, Mama, HIV
where I wanna be where i wanna be?
not where I AM

on the 102
down lex avenue
I do have
lungs take in air
I can see
I can read
nobody can see now
but I might be a poet, rapper, I got
  water colors
my child is smart
my CHILDREN
is alive
some girls in
forin countries
babies dead.
Look up sometimes
and the birds
is like dancers
or
like programmed
by computer
how they fly
tear up
your heart
bus moving
PLAY THE HAND YOU GOT
housemother say.

HOLD FAST TO DREAMS
Langston say.
GET UP OFF YOUR KNEES
Farrakhan say.
CHANGE
Alice Walker
say.
Rain fall down
wheels turn round
DON'T ALWAYS RHYME
Ms Rain say
walk on
go into the poem
the HEART of it
beating
like
a clock
a virus
tick
tock.

1991

Afterword

Sapphire

1.

THE BEGINNING

A poem is the harbinger of the novel to come. Then, as
now, a virus was upon the land:

I

```
. . . . . . . . . . . . . .
I am sorry I was out teacher.
My husband was sick.
You know I never miss school.
. . . . . . . . . . . . . .
What's wrong with my husband?
I don't know. He's in the
  hospital. He's real sick
I was almost out the room
When I hear the nurse ask him,
Do you do drugs?
He say yes.
```

AFTERWORD

I say what!
I don't know nuthin' 'bout no
    drugs.
. . . .
Huh?
Condoms? No, teacher.
He's my husband.
I never been with another man.

II

I think he got AIDS
he still don't tell me.
I did teacher. I tried
to read the chart at the
    hospital
but I couldn't figure out those
    words.
Doctor don't say, he say
    privacy.
The nurse tell me.
She's Puerto Rican. She say your
    husband
got AIDS.[1]

It's 1987. The class I'm teaching ends at noon. I try to encourage the students to come on time and to not leave early. A student gets up to leave. I put on a stern teacher face and glance at the clock, but she doesn't sit back down. "I have to leave early. I'm having trouble getting my AZT," she tells me. The statement stuns me. AZT? *She* has AIDS! This beautiful young Black woman has AIDS and she is having trouble getting the medication she needs to stay alive.[2] The AIDS epidemic as it affected Black women would be described in the mainstream media as a "silent epidemic" fueled by what white journalists would describe as "shame." But I was hearing, "I'm having trouble getting my AZT," in front of a classroom full of students. It wasn't the first time a student had put her life at center stage for us to see, braving stigma to shatter walls of silence and shame. This young woman put the word out. She, hence *we*, were in trouble, and she was facing obstacles getting the help she needed.

I will come to believe these obstacles had to do with her race and gender. Later I will make an observation in an interview: "Most of the people who have AIDS (HIV) are women of color, Black women, yet all of the economic resources to fight this disease are controlled by and directed toward the white gay male community downtown." Despite proclamations of my "misguided ignorance and homophobia" that were swift in coming, I was undeterred in this line of thought. I believed the federal, state, and city monies that flowed into the white male community were a lifeline that helped them

AFTERWORD

to survive. In the 1980s, a white man diagnosed with HIV/AIDS was many times more likely to survive than a Black woman diagnosed with the disease. Black women were often dead a week after diagnosis, while it was rumored that white men were somehow beginning to survive the diagnosis.

My student said, "I have to leave early. I'm having trouble getting my AZT." Later *The Wall Street Journal* published an article saying that the majority of people who have AIDS are women of color, but the majority of economic resources flow to, and are centered in, the white gay male community. I waited for a deluge of letters protesting the journalist's homophobia and his reliance on trumped-up statistics designed to deceive. If such protests ever came, I never saw them.

It is often posited that the AIDS epidemic first hit white gay men who were part of an intelligent and organized community, and that that is why white men began to suffer less mortality from AIDS than Black people. What I saw was organizing based on some of the tactics, strategies, and models of the civil rights movement: sit-ins, strikes, takeovers of public spaces, nonviolent (and sometimes violent) acting up, boycotts, etc. These were tactics that Black people used in the 1950s and '60s. Black women knew these strategies. It was posited that Black women suffered disproportionately from AIDS mortality because we didn't know how to organize, or because we were part of a "silent epidemic," or because we were on the "down-low" and riddled with shame—all of which may have been true, I don't know. But what I saw was that Black women were part of an underserved, devalued population from whom resources that could have saved our lives were being shunted.

A gay white supremacist said, "If there is to be a triage with these precious medicines (antivirals like AZT), they should go to white gay males who have contributed so much to society, and not to the blacks who don't even know what has hit them." When Andrew Sullivan said these words, he unequivocally upheld the racist belief that white gay males were worth more than Black people, and that if Black people were suffering disproportionately from AIDS, it was their own fault (i.e., because "they didn't know what hit them"). That most of the resources for education were being diverted downtown, where they were used to aid and educate white gay men (so they would know "what hit them"), did not seem to enter Sullivan's thinking. That Black people contributed as much or more to this country's culture and economy as white gay men and that Black people were as worthy as gay white males of receiving education and services that could help them understand the viral plague stalking the land did not cross this man's mind. (Decades later, echoes of this type of blame-the-victim racism and a YouTube video of Mayor Pete Buttigieg— the first openly gay presidential candidate—making a birther joke about President Obama, doomed, in my opinion, his chance of getting any widespread support in the Black community for his presidential bid.)

The current situation in 2020–21 has parallels to the one I faced twenty-five years ago—a virus was upon the land, disproportionately killing Black people whose access to information or ability to process information because of educational deficiencies was not as it should have been. The Centers for Disease Control and Prevention (CDC) issued report after report in 2020 echoing a devastating finding: the SARS-CoV-2 virus that causes COVID-19 was hitting Black people hard. That came as no surprise. There has hardly been a disease that has not hit Black people harder than it has white people. Reports show that some of the populations, including Black communities, that were hit hardest by COVID-19, indeed, did not know what hit them. But the suggested response was not to divert resources from those communities; it was, instead, to educate them. And according to a *New York Times* article, while COVID-19 did hit poor, Latinx, Black, and other communities with preexisting conditions hard, *where* people were treated also seemed to make a difference. Certain hospitals, "safety-net" hospitals, where dark-skinned minorities and low-income people often ended up, had far worse patient outcomes than wealthier hospitals; that is, despite lower socioeconomic status and preexisting conditions, dark-skinned minorities often survived when admitted to wealthier hospitals, but when admitted to safety-net hospitals, they died.

Saying I was observing a vastly uneven playing field would be an understatement. The words that came to mind then, as now, were Jonathan Kozol's *savage inequalities*.

The inability to access health care services and educational opportunities deprived and stunted the lives of students like those described in my novel *PUSH*, which was based, in part, on my experiences teaching in New York City. Though my students' studies were sometimes focused on very rudimentary skills, all my students were at least sixteen, and most were adults, eighteen years old and up. Most of my students received some type of public assistance, and the programs I taught in the Bronx, Harlem, and Brooklyn were educational ones.

The political rhetoric being disseminated in low tones at the time was discouraging, disparaging, and had been around for a while, but it was about to get loud. It would sound like the castigations that were to ooze out of the likes of Newt Gingrich as he bullied the poor, with a particular focus on Black women receiving Aid to Families with Dependent Children (AFDC) benefits, or what is commonly called welfare.

"How can a seventeen-year-old with a baby be considered a family?" conservatives opined from public podiums. What they meant is, How could state and federal governments, we the people, justify giving aid (a welfare check) to people like my students—people who had babies out of "wedlock"; people who needed to be punished, not rewarded; people who needed to be married, or at home with their parents, or at one of the boarding schools that the Republican Party talked about building as a very concrete way of containerizing the teenage mothers and any other young women seeking public assistance to establish a household outside of the conservatives' idea of where a young woman should be, which was at her parents' house or at her husband's house. The idea that poverty, which by some counts at the time affected two-thirds of African Americans, was caused by a runaway, errant female sexuality that bred irresponsibly was a miscreant notion disseminated by Daniel Patrick Moynihan and others, promulgated by Gingrich and the like, and accepted by Bill Clinton.

The idea that there was an almost ironclad caste system based on race, ingrained in the very fiber of the nation's being, and that that caste system upheld, and was upheld by, the rampant destruction of Black families through the imprisonment of Black men, was somehow beyond their comprehension. To my thinking, it was just inconvenient, because accepting that Black poverty is the result of racism would have meant attacking individual and institutional racism. It was so much easier to attack a poor Black single mother's personhood and imagined hyperfertility—which unfortunately sometimes resulted in attacks upon her *actual* fertility, in the form of coerced sterilizations and in some states the withholding of food, shelter, and other benefits from women who refused "control of" or "to control" their fertility and continued to have children while receiving public assistance.

"How can a seventeen-year-old with a baby be considered a family?" My answer to that highly partisan question is to ask another question: How can a seventeen-year-old with a baby *not* be considered a family? How can she not be considered a head of household? In the programs I taught, I encountered these young adults daily—desperate for the skills to survive, eager to learn how to care for and hold on to their children, and determined not to see their children disappear in the dark hole of foster care only to come out eighteen years later, like some of them had, uneducated and homeless, struggling with a government more willing to pay to containerize them and to give money to foster care agencies to raise their children than to give to young mothers directly the money necessary to feed, clothe, house, and educate their children and themselves.

2.

EDUCATION AS RESISTANCE

Some of the women I taught in those years came to the program from homeless shelters. They were coming from halfway houses after having been incarcerated. They were coming to class after being laid off from jobs. Sometimes they were in rehab; sometimes they came from stable homes in which they had in the past made the choice to put caregiving over getting an education. They came with bad vision; they came sharp-eyed. They came with bad teeth and with million-dollar smiles. They came documented and undocumented, docile and defiant.

What they found in me was a woman whose Holy Grail was certain academic studies that said the same thing over and over, in many different ways, at many different times. These studies were consistent, but they got little oxygen in any political climate, conservative or liberal. They were the light in the darkness in which I labored.

The darkness was the vast, horrible, historic disservice of the Moynihan Report, which somehow saw the strength of the Black single mother who was head of household as a problem. And declared that Black poverty did not stem from the consistent and brutal deprivation of access to education, health care, and business opportunities by a white power structure that worked systemically, institutionally, and personally to deprive Black people of the fruits of American society (all the while, and most especially, not acknowledging that those fruits were derived from the very people deprived of those fruits). The Moynihan Report did not see the increasing numbers of incarcerated Black people (male and female) as having anything to do with what he saw as the destruction of the Black family.

What Moynihan saw as the problem was the Black

woman, who, by hook or by crook, managed to eke out some kind of survival on public assistance (welfare), and that this ability to survive, this reliance on public assistance, had caused the Black male's absence from the Black family. Hence the Black family found itself pathologically (and antipatriarchally) headed by women. In looking at the problems poor Black people faced, mass incarceration and racist exclusions from every area of opportunity in American life were not addressed as causal factors—these things were not even really acknowledged. But what *was* addressed was Black women's reliance on public assistance.

I write this now having a great chronological, intellectual, and emotional distance from the younger idealistic woman who read the studies in the 1980s and 1990s. I don't have access to the file cabinets of articles, the notebooks filled with class notes, the lesson plans, the student diaries, the student materials I used to compile and write, my "urban intellectual guerrilla research"[3]—but that research and lived experience refuted Moynihan, Gingrich, and Clinton, who set in motion such devastating policies as "three strikes and you do life" and other nonsensical and cruel legislation that had the effect of locking African American men and women away for the rest of their lives. These policies were so egregious and deserving of attention that other equally harmful policies of that administration, which continued the previous regime's policies of blaming the victims for their poverty, escaped notice.

My students and I knew that their poverty was the result of a race, class, and gender system skewed against them. They were poor and uneducated by design, from de facto segregated school systems to gender discrimination and violence. The system was not just stacked against them; it was falling down upon them and crushing them.

The Clinton administration decided not to increase educational opportunities for women on public assistance and to end those that existed (like the ones I was teaching in) by having them segue into job-training programs. The administration decided not to implement more programs to end gender-based violence and to cease supporting the ones already in existence. The administration decided that public assistance was the biggest problem for women living in poverty, and that the government subsidies for rent, soap and diapers for their babies, and food stamps for beans, rice, milk, soda, and beef—these subsidies were what needed to be eliminated, not poverty. So, Clinton decided to "end welfare as we know it," and if his other policies locked up Black men and threw the key farther away than it had ever been, his administration's welfare "reform" law plunged some women and children deeper into financial distress, evictions, food insecurity, prostitution, homelessness, drug use, and despair than they had ever been under the previous regime.

At my first teaching jobs, I made twelve to fourteen dollars an hour in places that were often referred to as off-site, meaning they might have been affiliated with a university department or a community-based organization that got a grant to teach a class located in a low-income urban community—which could sound progressive, right? *In the community?* But when it was off-site, it effectively kept us out of sight. It also kept us from libraries, computer labs, gyms, clean restrooms, and lounges that "regular" students used. Bringing school to the community was decidedly not the same as bringing the community to school. But it was something. Clinton's welfare "reform" law was intending to pull us out of even the substandard facilities we had had and put the women who attended the educational programs to work. And oftentimes not for money but in exchange for their check, their so-called handout from the government, which was tainted with overtones of charity instead of an acknowledgment of a racist system kept in place by the subjugation and exploitation of poor people and people of color.

Our programs provided hope, and you could see it at our graduation ceremonies as women displayed newfound skills: how to open a bank or checking account (no more fees at the check-cashing establishment); how to fill out a job application; how to get into a GED class, or go from a GED class to a community or four-year college. I believe this blow against poor women by a government that subsidized corporations didn't only cost these women a chance to advance—for some, I believe it was deadly. I believe it cost them their lives.

AFTERWORD

The light in my heart, the studies that were ignored and made obscure, was what I used to guide my actions. The government wanted us to shunt the women toward jobs or workfare—*workfare* being unpaid work that the women would do in exchange for whatever government assistance they were receiving, be it food stamps, AFDC (Aid to Families with Dependent Children), or Medicaid. Workfare recipients could be on street-cleaning crews or be office clerks—all this work, of course, supplanting union jobs (who can beat people working for free!). But these jobs didn't last. They weren't jobs, per se; they were punishments for being poor, they were paying the system back for having received benefits to stave off hunger and homelessness. Something almost always went wrong on these jobs. The most disturbing was the physical violence sometimes inflicted upon them by paid workers whose jobs they were usurping. And the jobs were stigmatized. Other workers knew they were welfare recipients being "put to work" because welfare as we knew it had ended.

Everything had failed with these women. Recidivism was common; many workers would return to welfare after having attained minimum-wage jobs. But the studies I had read—my Holy Grail—talked of a way, *the one way*, that did not fail. And that was with *education*. The researchers said that when women received a college education, they, in the great majority of cases, came off public assistance (welfare) of any kind for the rest of their lives.

What my students needed was an *education*, not to be sweeping the streets or shunted into homeless shelters or kicked off welfare for coming to school instead of going to their workfare jobs, because the one thing shown to permanently remove women from the welfare rolls was a college education. It was my mantra:

> The one thing shown to permanently remove women from welfare rolls is a college education. The one thing shown to permanently remove women from welfare rolls is a college education. The one thing shown to permanently remove women from welfare rolls is a college education. The one thing shown . . .

In that dark time, it was the light under which I labored. But most of the educational programs I taught in would be shuttered under the Clinton administration. *I* would be the one going on to university, not the women in our programs. I continued to teach as I sought an advanced degree, but never again would I teach women like the ones who made up the "girlz" in the novel *PUSH*. We were separated by government policy and our own shifting fortunes, but they remain alive in my heart—a moment of time preserved in the two-way journals readers encounter in my novel.

It's 2020, and I'm in lockdown in downtown Brooklyn because of COVID-19. I would like to show you, but I cannot put my hands on the letters that came to me via my publisher, my agent, and my teaching colleagues, stuffed in individual envelopes and in large manila envelopes. They came from regular folks in book clubs, educators who assigned *PUSH* in their classes, and scholars who wrote papers on *PUSH*— people who were touched by a girl whose life (thankfully) had been nothing like their own. And people whose lives (sorrowfully) had been much like Precious's but who wanted me to know that they, too, like her, had survived. There were poets and artists struck by the ferocious-crazy-quilt-female artistry displayed in a book that promoted colored female collectivity and caring over competition. This was a caring that had historically been diverted from the Black community and distorted and usurped to nurture, bolster, and build up the Upper West Sides of New York and the world. High-income white nuclear families demanded the low-paid labor provided by "nigger" and Hispanic nannies and maids—not too different from the way whites during slavery and the years following the abolition of slavery furiously demanded the mother-nurture and female energy of the Black family, first for nonpaid labor and then for low-paid domestic work, labor that enabled white families to rise and helped keep "niggers" in their place. Between the murder, harassment, and imprisonment of Black men and the derailment of Black women into service, the lower-class status of some Black people was often effectively sealed. This was so common, it was just understood: Black female energy was to be diverted for the raising and nurturing of our oppressors, keeping Black people in poverty while elevating the financial and emotional well-being of those for whom Black people were forced to or had little choice but to serve.

In *PUSH*, spectacularly, we see that energy being used by women of color, most specifically Black women, for their own nurturance and their own spiritual and educational ascent, which holds within it the possibility of a step up from the bottom rung of the economic ladder in those—*these!*—savagely unequal and divided United States of America.

Think of what America had seen before the film *Precious: Based on the Novel* PUSH *by Sapphire*, when they encountered an obese dark-skinned Black woman on the screen—Hattie McDaniel, Louise Beavers, etc. If these characters had—as Precious does—inner lives, sexual fantasies, romantic reveries, or ambition ("but I might be a poet, rapper," says a radicalized Precious in *PUSH*), they were never shown. What was shown were neutered and loyal workhorses whose loyalties were to the family they worked for and maybe even lived with, either because of the total devotion needed to raise and nurture the white family's children or because they did not earn enough to ever live independently.

In both the novel and the film, Precious's formidable intelligence, beauty, and potential do not revolve around upper-class white women who need her labor

AFTERWORD

to achieve their feminist longings. And though the system urges her to cease her education long before she even knows how to spell the word *college* so that she can become a home attendant, Precious resists. "No way!" Precious says. "I'm getting my G.E.D., a job . . . then I go to college."

3.

SAPPHIRE'S LITERARY BREAKTHROUGH

Sapphire's Literary Breakthrough: Erotic Literacies, Feminist Pedagogies, Environmental Justice Perspectives, edited by Elizabeth McNeil, Neal A. Lester, DoVeanna S. Fulton, and Lynette D. Myles, is a collection of essays that author and professor Sonja L. Lanehart hailed as "a welcome addition to African American literary criticism." Author and professor Trudier Harris praised it by saying, "While these essays are assuredly rooted in solid scholarship, they are equally rooted in loving appreciation for a groundbreaking artist." And according to Ronald L. Jackson II, author of *Masculinity in the Black Imagination*, this "rich set of essays . . . lay[s] bare the fragility of Black lives."

How did this collection of essays come about? We can get an idea by reading DoVeanna S. Fulton's essay "Looking for 'the Alternative[s]': Locating Sapphire's

PUSH in African American Literary Tradition through Literacy and Orality," where she notes:

> A search of the Modern Language Association [MLA] *Bibliography* yields eight articles and book chapters on the text [*PUSH*], mostly focused on survivor narratives and the clinical uses of narrative as therapeutic device.[4]

Fulton goes on to quote Rafia Zafar:

> "We should not depend on what materials the MLA *Bibliography* includes to estimate scholarly attention, nor should we confuse the so-called center of academic discourse with the sum of intellectual work." Certainly the MLA *Bibliography* is not exhaustive; however, as the premier database for literary scholarship, it does point to the broad scholarly community consciousness. Yet this circumstance is unfortunate and unmerited for *PUSH*, because this novel is clearly situated within African American literary tradition. Sapphire mines and reconfigures major tropes and motifs found in the large body of African American literature to produce a work that is both familiar and asks critics to consider these tropes in new ways for twentieth-century readers.[5]

I think this was one of the convictions that brought these scholars together. Professor Elizabeth McNeil,

AFTERWORD

author of *Trickster Discourse: Mediating Transformation for a New World* and *Ms. X's Ocean*, focuses her work on multiethnic women's science and literature, ecofeminist approaches to literature, "freak" studies in literature and film, and transgender and intersex literature and film. DoVeanna S. Fulton, provost and vice president for academic affairs at Norfolk State University, is the author of *Speaking Power: Black Feminist Orality in Women's Narratives of Slavery* and coeditor with Reginald H. Pitts of *Speaking Lives, Authoring Texts: Three African American Women's Oral Slave Narratives*. Neal A. Lester, Foundation Professor of English at Arizona State University, is the author of *Ntozake Shange: A Critical Study of the Plays* and *Understanding Zora Neal Hurston's* Their Eyes Were Watching God: *A Student Casebook to Issues, Sources, and Historical Documents* and is coeditor of *Racialized Politics of Desire in Personal Ads*. Professor Lynette D. Myles is the author of *Female Subjectivity in African American Women's Narratives of Enslavement: Beyond Borders*, including the essay "At the Crossroads of Black Female Autonomy, or Digression as Resistance in *Quicksand* and *The Street*." Was it their conviction to challenge, as Professor Fulton writes, the sway of the MLA, which, situated in and reflective of the Northeast, indicates by its inclusion or exclusion which works are worthy of study, which works will live, and which will die?

If so, what followed was, to my thinking, a revolutionary act.

It began in February 2007 with a symposium hosted by Professors McNeil, Myles, Fulton, and Neal that was held at Arizona State University. Scholars, students, faculty, and other members of the Arizona State University community joined with scholars and students who traveled from around the country to present papers on my books *PUSH*, *American Dreams*, and *Black Wings & Blind Angels*. The volume *Sapphire's Literary Breakthrough* grew from this conference.

In *The Complete Autobiographies of Frederick Douglass*, Frederick Douglass, for the most part, did not spend a lot of ink on the plight of the female slave who is sexually victimized. This is the void that Harriet Jacobs takes up in *Incidents in the Life of a Slave Girl*. There had been almost no place in African American literary fiction—or in any other kind of African American literature—before *PUSH*, which explored some of the difficult truths of early childhood sexual abuse, such as the female as perpetrator and the body as a site of pleasure even when being abused. Many mainstream reviewers gave credence to the novel's literary value, and for some this was *despite* the attention the novel gave to what one described as "over-the-top" subject matter. Some of the reviewers questioned the necessity of exploring subject matter like mother-daughter genital incest in print, stating that it detracted from the text.

Sometime in the late 1990s, an avant-garde theater artist approached me about doing a stage adaptation of *PUSH*, which she did beautifully. But she said to me at the beginning: "Sapphire, you know that scene with the mother?" She was referring to a scene in which mother-daughter incest is depicted. "Don't worry; we're going to leave it out."

The scholars contributing to *Sapphire's Literary Breakthrough* move in for a more nuanced analysis, realizing the so-called over-the-top depictions of sexual abuse do not detract from the text's literary value, but *add* to it. Elizabeth McNeil notes in her essay "Deconstructing the 'Pedagogy of Abuse': Teaching Child Sexual Abuse Narratives":

> As a personal and politically relevant text, *PUSH* is an incest narrative that includes details of child sexual abuse that have thus far been generally avoided in this feminist literary genre: the confusing reality of sexual stimulation during unwanted incestuous intercourse, and mother-daughter incest.[6]

In L. H. Stallings's essay "Sapphire's *PUSH* for Erotic Literacy and Black Girl Sexual Agency," the author notes:

> Mary [Precious's mother] does not desire Precious in the same manner as the father desires daughter in any incest narrative to date in African American literary tradition. Mary's abuse is a revenge enacted against competition. . . .
>
> . . . Sapphire moves beyond [Hortense] Spillers's

theory that "the legends of incest are 'male-identified,' phallogocentrally determined," [. . .] beyond the missing/absent mother who plays a role in the drama of father-daughter incest. With each learning invocation, new narratives are formed. What happens with Mary's sexual abuse of Precious is something more than incest, and the key impetus is a complicit understanding, specifically black women's and black mothers' complicity in upholding the Father's law. Mary is not absent or missing [during the abuse of Precious by her father]. She stays, she watches, and she participates in the erasure of another female's agency. Thus, when the father goes missing/absent, Sapphire shapes her collusion and allows it to turn Mary into a perpetrator.[7]

Along these lines, McNeil notes:

Critics and clinicians note that *PUSH*'s point-of-view protagonist, Precious Jones, shows a much more developed sense of agency than does Pecola Breedlove, the silent, abused girl at the heart of the key predecessor text, Toni Morrison's *The Bluest Eye* (1970). [. . .] In "Agents of Pain and Redemption in Sapphire's *PUSH*," Janice Lee Liddell, writing in 1999, remarks that "By giving voice to the victim herself—a phenomenon virtually unheard of in Black sociological, psychological, or imaginative

literature—the root causes of the incest are inter-
rogated and the agency of this violence is spread
as far as possible." From *The Bluest Eye* to *PUSH*
marks an evolution in our late-twentieth-century
ability to see the survivor of incest, child sexual
abuse, or rape as someone who has a legitimate
place in society. . . .

Offering a greater sense of the affected character's agency than does Morrison's earlier *The Bluest Eye*, *PUSH* affords the reader an even greater
possibility [. . .] to respond and react to Sapphire's
more complex understanding of that lived experience. The specific ways that Sapphire creates a
more intimate and relevant incest story include
the unusual mother-daughter incest and Precious's
confusing sexual responses. Even more signifi-
cantly, as critics note, in *PUSH* and *The Bluest Eye*,
whereas Precious articulates her abuse story from
the first sentence of the novel, Pecola's story is only
told by others.

Liddell asserts that, unlike other earlier African American writers who have "tiptoed through
taboo," Sapphire forcefully confronts the issue of
incest in the black community, and thereby creates
"the atmosphere and the mechanisms for real and
significant transformation . . ." In going beyond
what Morrison, in *The Bluest Eye*, and Alice Walker,
in her short fiction and, most notably, *The Color
Purple* (1982), had done for an earlier generation

of readers and students, Sapphire, in *PUSH*, "has gone far," Liddell asserts, "in transforming the literary consciousness of African Americans."[8]

Many detractors and some admirers of the novel only saw a dysfunctional inner-city landscape, a terrain of danger and disease. They didn't see that this landscape could shift into and coexist simultaneously with creativity, healing, and sanctuary—as it does in *PUSH*. Lynette D. Myles notes in her brilliant book *Female Subjectivity in African American Women's Narratives of Enslavement*, "Black women shift from locations they once retreated into—insanity—to sites that allow both growth and development."[9] That shift can happen with a *word* or its redefinition; poet Lucille Clifton demonstrates so lucidly in her poem "in the inner city" that what *they* call one thing, *we* call another. What *they* call "inner city," *we* call "home."[10]

Inner city signifies an imperiled existence, but *home* is a signifier of safety. The novel I wrote challenges the idea that for so-called marginalized communities the only hope is white intervention and/or escape. In the very environment where Precious is so horribly abused and neglected are the resources and spirit/souls capable of helping her survive. Elizabeth McNeil notes in her essay "Un-'Freak'ing Black Female Self: Grotesque-Erotic Agency and Ecofeminist Unity in Sapphire's *PUSH*":

> As Precious becomes a member of her learning community at Each One Teach One [ten blocks from her home], she emerges from depression and begins to notice both her body/her nature and the environment she inhabits. . . . At her new school, Precious generates her transformative self-reunification by finally voicing her illiteracy and allowing Ms. Rain to teach her how to read.[11]

Precious is not "other" to Ms. Rain. The reader will remember that this "reunification with the self," which ultimately leads to the ability to "voice," did not happen with Precious's white male teacher Mr. Wicher, whom Precious adores but who only tolerates her and uses her to keep order in a classroom he does not have the skills to control. He indeed sees her as a "grotesque," if he sees her at all.

When we help ourselves to Joni Adamson's analysis in "'Spiky Green Life': Environmental, Food, and Sexual Justice Themes in Sapphire's *PUSH*," we see the "bleak ghetto" landscape as mutable. We see not just the horror but the wonder:

> "mornin/if you/like/me/you see/ILANATHA tree rape/concreet/n birf/spiky green/trunk/life." This miraculous "spiky green/trunk/life" has deep significance for Precious; the emerging tree, coming up through the concrete, stands as a powerful symbol for the *social justice and greening* [emphasis

mine] projects that real-world grassroots groups are organizing in communities like Harlem. . . .

. . . [Ms. Rain] tells the class to bring "something of YOU" into the classroom. Precious brings a picture of her son Abdul and a live "plant from Woolworth on 125th Street." . . . She writes about her plant in her journal: "It growed. Leaves big." . . . The thriving plant reflects Precious's growing intellectual and environmental literacy and symbolizes the importance of bright, living environments.[12]

There were questions raised about whether *PUSH* could be taught and, more important, *how*, given the content and the context of African American literature classes in a white- and male-dominated environment. Neal A. Lester addresses these questions in "'Rock the Motherfucking House': Guiding a Study of Sapphire's *PUSH*":

Too often, controversial texts are not taught regularly in the classroom because teachers themselves are not confident enough to engage their students in discussion of the recognizably challenging and sensitive subject matter.[13]

What follows in Lester's essay is to date not just the most thorough pedagogical guide to teaching *PUSH* but also a guide that can be adapted, I believe, to teach any work that lies outside of almost any teacher's self-perceived abilities to render a text meaningful to students' experiences. This consummate scholar made sure that while he was the first in the room to provide this intrepid analysis and pedagogical guide (I hear Vice President Kamala Harris expounds on what it means to be the first in the room!), one of the many firsts in his long academic career, he would not be the last—that is, if others have the courage to follow.

4.

THE MOVIE

The first people who approached me about film rights were successful Hollywood producers from major studios. Friends could not understand why I would turn down these offers. But I wanted the book to have a chance to breathe, to exist in people's minds and imaginations. I wanted what happens when you read—the words coming into your mind through the eye, the ear, the fingertips. An image is produced, depending on the storyteller's ability and the reader's emotional, imaginative, and intellectual range of motion. One reader told me that after reading *PUSH*, she saw the longing and beauty of Precious everywhere in faces that were formerly invisible to her. One older white man said he would never look at women who looked "like that" in the same way. That was part of what I wanted.

Then independent directors and producers—white and Black—started coming to me. A young Black director wrote and said he was ready! And that as far as who would play the part of Precious was concerned, I was not to worry. He had Brandy, the pop and R&B star, on call and ready to go. I said that I appreciated Brandy's talent, but I wanted someone who looks like the character in the book. He told me, *Sapphire, there are no people in Hollywood who look like the character in the book*.

That was twenty-five years ago. Now there are people who look like Precious in Hollywood. In fact, they were *always* there, but as I mentioned earlier, for the most part they played roles, sometimes with great dignity and talent and humor, of women forced into enabling, through their labor, an oppressive caste system that elevates white women, white men, and their white offspring. The servants they played on-screen were desexualized subservient second-class citizens trapped in low-wage work that allowed the whites who employed them to rise. The movies I grew up watching showed Black women who look like Louise Beaver, Hattie McDaniel, and me laboring in and building a world from which we were excluded. We cleaned the lakeshore homes and penthouse apartments; we cooked and served and changed diapers and had children palmed off on us to raise. Read almost any upper-class white memoir of a certain era and you will be told about a mammy or colored nurse or Negro maid whom they loved and gave their old clothes to, etc. And they will fight you if you suggest to them that maybe they were not loved by said servant in kind. That this assumed love took place as its recipients often grew up to undermine affirmative action and/or to lobby against the unionization of household workers, and how the "beloved" caregiver's own children were sidelined or pipelined to prison is rarely part of the story.

It would take the genius of Lee Daniels to present a Black female who looks like Precious as a *child* and to depict a childhood that ascends from one of horror to one of hopes and dreams. Much has been said about the movie *Precious*, most of it very good. *Precious* received worldwide accolades and dozens of nominations in many award categories, including six Academy Award nominations. Lee Daniels won the People's Choice Award at the Toronto International Film Festival and the TVE Otra Mirada Award and the Audience Award at the San Sebastián International Film Festival. He received an Academy Award nomination for Best Director. Actress Mo'Nique received more than sixty nominations for her supporting role as Precious's mother and won many, including an Oscar, a Golden Globe, and a BAFTA Award for Best Supporting Actress. At the Stockholm International Film Festival, where there is no Best Supporting Actress category, Mo'Nique straight-up won Best Actress.

When an author and a director enter into an agreement to make a film, there is a transaction far more consequential than the legal contract, the financial arrangement, or even the decisions about representation and interpretation. There is an issue of trust. For me, the trust I put in Lee Daniels was simple: I trusted him to make a work of art, and he never wavered. In my opinion, and in agreement with A. O. Scott of the *New York Times*, *Precious* is a genuine work of art.

While no work is above criticism, some of the criticism *Precious* received was truly baffling to me and, I believe, missed the point of the work completely. One well-known Black male writer commented in the *New York Times* on the Blackness of Gabourey Sidibe, who plays Precious in the film, how dark her dark skin is compared with the light-skinned Blackness of actress Paula Patton, who plays the teacher. Was he forgetting the very real class divide based on skin color among Black people? Dark-skinned Blacks typically receive longer prison sentences than light-skinned Blacks convicted of the same crime; marriage rates among dark-skinned Blacks are lower than they are among light-skinned Blacks; and for a long time, light-skinned Blacks were more likely to be educated and to become doctors and teachers—like the teacher depicted in the film.

Another male writer, a Black nationalist, wrote an op-ed in the *New York Times* denouncing the on-screen display of what he labeled "Black pathology"[14]—most specifically, what he viewed as the perpetuation of racist stereotypes, in that the main character is raped by her father, who is a Black man.

He wrote a near-full-page editorial, stating that the type of violence depicted against the film's main character, Precious, was unbelievable, a stereotyping of Black men, and a misrepresentation of Black culture. While I myself reject the labeling of pathological behavior as Black pathology, I do not reject the fact that Black people can and do act pathologically toward each other. I reject the view that those actions are inherently Black in any way. I contacted the *Times* and asked to address his attack in my own op-ed. I was told that they did not publish editorials in response to editorials, but I could reply in a letter to the editor, which has a strict word count.

The published op-ed to which I felt the need to respond covered very familiar territory: *you-Black-women-make-us-Black-males-look-bad-by-talking-about-how-we-raped-you-YOU-are-bad-for-saying-we-raped-you-and-white-people-are-bad-for-printing-stories-about-Black-males-raping-Black-females-and-Black-children-and-fyi-what-you-whites-should-publish-are-accounts-of-WHITE-people-abusing-Black-people*, etc., etc., etc.

The problem with telling someone not to talk about what has happened to them is that what has happened to them is their story. It's a *part* of them, and to silence their telling is an act of erasure. We see it happen all the time—a victim's story gets replaced with that of the victimizer. The story of the heroic German non-Jewish

Nazi resister; the valiant white woman slaveholder; the employer of a brown domestic laborer who becomes the hero and usurps the victim's story. Usurping the victim's story and replacing it with a narrative in which the oppressor is the hero gives back to the oppressor, illegitimately, the humanity that they lost when they raped, murdered, culturally appropriated, and/or economically exploited someone. What right does an accused group or individual have to cut out the tongue of the one who accuses because the accusation is making the accused look bad or disrupts their own victim narrative?

This is the letter I wrote that appeared in the *New York Times*:

> Re "Fade to White": In the 13 years since my novel "*PUSH*" was published, I have talked to thousands of women who have been sexually abused, some of whom have had experiences that make what happened in *PUSH*, which was made into the film "*Precious: Based on the Novel 'PUSH' by Sapphire*," look like a walk in the park.
>
> I'm not a social scientist but a creative artist. I took and will continue to take the stories of women I have listened to and turn them into fiction.
>
> I write about black women because it's the world I know. "Fade to White" mentions that incest is not confined to one group of people. I

agree, but I argue that it does have a different
place in African-American culture than it has in
white American culture. During slavery many
black women were impregnated by their masters,
who were often also their fathers. The white male
was literally the master-father of the plantation.

I would like to see black males less defensive
and more courageous in their investigations of
sexual abuse in the black community. I would
like to see more, not less, written about rape by
African-Americans.

African-Americans have the highest rate
of heterosexual H.I.V. infection in the United
States. While the effects of sexual abuse are
traumatic for any group of women, black women
more often than any other ethnic group must
deal with being infected with H.I.V. by our
perpetrators.

Silence will not save African-Americans.
We've got to work hard and long, and our work
begins by telling our stories out loud to whoever
has the courage to listen.[15]

I believe the op-ed to which I responded was an attempt
by the writer to silence my work, because he believed
that showing so graphically the abuse of a Black woman-
child disrupts the Black-male-as-victim narrative. Actually, it doesn't, but I believe that's the operative belief
in trying to silence Black women's narratives of abuse.

My response was promptly published by the *New York Times*.

Because of space consideration, my letter had to be edited. This is common, but it's still interesting now to look at what they chose to take out:

> He (the [slave] master) had sex with whom he
> wanted to: black women, children, AND men.
> This was the "family" structure most slaves were
> exposed to. Black men were not allowed to act
> out the role of father. They themselves were
> raped like women, in addition to being turned
> into stud-like breeders. We as a race have yet to
> deal with the fact that black men were raped like
> "bitches" during slavery; nor have we dealt with
> the impact that that has had on the generations of
> us that came out of slavery.

Looking back, I believe what was edited out is a far bigger story than what was printed. And the question arises: Who gets to tell that story? Printing those sentences in my letter to the editor would have taken the dialogue to another level, addressing not just how the Black male writer felt he looked to white people in a screen depiction of what he saw as a pathological portrayal of Black manhood, but also the incarnation of the American institution of slavery, which rooted itself in the belief of the supremacy of the so-called white race and the subhuman status of Black people. And it is this belief that we, and the world, suffer from and struggle with to this day.

The pathology the op-ed writer fears being associated with is incest, well described in Black literature from *The Invisible Man* to *The Bluest Eye*. These are the stories from our geniuses. Then there are stories in broken and humbler but no less courageous language, in the journal entries of psych-ward patients, the testimonies of women in therapist offices and recovery groups—and they tell the same stories of the pathological abuse of power through forced sex.

What was done to George Floyd was done in broad daylight, with the perpetrator knowing he was being recorded. When George Floyd complained that he couldn't breathe, he was told, "It takes energy to talk." In other words, "Shut up!" If this can happen in eight minutes and forty-six seconds in broad daylight, we can only imagine what happened in the hundreds of years of slavery. To say that there weren't and aren't positive, life-giving aspects in Black culture is a denial tantamount to the racism that caused us to be used so cruelly for so long. But when we read about the epigenetic changes in the children of Holocaust survivors, should we not consider that psychological, physical, and even genetic responses to slavery rapes and neoslavery rapes should be examined as part of post-traumatic slave syndrome?

The stories in *PUSH* of girls like Precious are not unusual. It was at Bronx Community College that a student in my Adult Basic Education (ABE) class, at first, confused me. I knew she was thirty-three years old—at some point she told me, or I knew it from looking at her intake information. One day she mentioned that she had to pick up her daughter and that said daughter was twenty years old. The numbers were jarring. If she had a twenty-year-old daughter . . . Evidently knowing what I was thinking, she said, "I had a baby by my father when I was thirteen years old, and she has Down's syndrome."

She was intelligent and articulate, and it always seemed to me that we could have easily changed places—she, the teacher; me, the student. I had wondered what happened, how she ended up in a class like this one. Now I knew, or at least I had a powerful clue. This woman did not "become" Precious, but that sad fact of her life informed the story I chose to write and went into the unique character of Precious, a child of my imagination.

In the 1980s, AIDS was thought of by many as a white gay disease, but that idea changed rapidly. A gay publication almost triumphantly announced how well the gay community had done with containing AIDS, that AIDS was now *just* a Black disease.

You could hear a collective sigh of relief then, twenty-five years ago, as you can now, in 2021, that COVID-19 has bypassed some Americans and fallen down hard on others, especially Black and brown people. (Excess deaths among Black and Hispanic people of all ages also rose in 2020, compared with 2019's rate—33 percent rise in Blacks and 54 percent rise in Hispanics, respectively. Among whites, the increase in deaths was only 12 percent, according to an October 2020 report from the CDC.)[16]

COVID-19, like all diseases, hits hardest the poor, the people of color, and the socially vulnerable—people who are incarcerated, who live communally, who live in nursing homes. As affirmative action continues to be attacked, poor Black people have found and will consistently find themselves in contact with doctors who, for the most part, are white or Asian American, some of whom are totally clueless—often because it serves them to be—of the racist American caste system; doctors who believe they are in their position because they worked hard, while the people whom they are watching die, who have had centuries of unearned contempt dumped upon them, are dying at exponentially faster rates because they do not work hard. They with their great educations are ignorant of the Precious ones whom they should be serving, often contributing to higher death rates by their sometimes clueless—and sometimes knowing—participation in medical and institutional racism. As one African American woman quoted in the *New York Times* put it, "When we get to the hospital, they treat us different." How could they not?

The African American experience is the fourth dimension to an immigrant who believes there is no caste system in America and that he got to where he is

because he "worked very hard." The same challenges
of race and caste which beset us twenty-five years ago
beset us now, when things should be so much better.
And, like twenty-five years ago, the people now dying
and being dumped in unmarked or mass graves were
employed in professions like mine and looked like me
and like the people I taught.

I write this afterword in a mournful time. It is a
dirge. I write this afterword in a time of an undeclared
and much-denied war upon my people, the people of
PUSH, the people of mass graves and the rainbow of
Black-yellow-beige-red-brown-disenfranchised-and-
uninsured, the people upon whom the weight of this
rabid, racist, and very uncivil civilization called America
has fallen. I write this afterword as a war cry, a double-
edged ax against our annihilation and erasure.

This afterword began with a poem. *PUSH* ends with
a poem, a vocalization of impending danger and fierce
hope:

```
                untitled
          by Precious Jones


    Rain, wheels, bus
    car,
    only in dreams
    I have car
    me n Abdul riding like
    in the movies
```

sun a yellow red ball
rising over hills
where indiens usta live
beaches, Islands
where Jamaica talks live
Bob Marley
song
first I don't unnerstan it
but now I do
CONCREET JUNGLE
it's a prison days
we live in
at least me
I'm not really free
baby, Mama, HIV
where I wanna be where i wanna
   be?
not where I AM
. . . .
Look up sometimes
and the birds
is like dancers
or
like programmed
by computer
how they fly
tear up
your heart
bus moving

. . . .
CHANGE
Alice Walker
say.
Rain fall down
wheels turn round
. . . .
walk on
go into the poem
the HEART of it
beating
like
a clock
a virus
tick
tock.

Notes

1. Sapphire, *Black Wings & Blind Angels* (New York: Alfred A. Knopf, 1999), 95–96.

2. In those days the word *AIDS* was sometimes mistakenly and confusingly used interchangeably with *HIV positive*.

3. See "Introduction," in *Vernaculars in the Classroom: Paradoxes, Pedagogy, Possibilities* by Shondel Nero and Dohra Ahmad (New York: Routledge, 2014).

4. DoVeanna S. Fulton, "Looking for 'the Alternative[s]': Locating Sapphire's *PUSH* in African American Literary Tradition through Literacy and Orality," in *Sapphire's Literary Breakthrough: Erotic Literacies, Feminist Pedagogies, Environmental Justice Perspectives*, ed. Elizabeth McNeil, Neal A. Lester, DoVeanna S. Fulton, and Lynette D. Myles (New York/London: Palgrave Macmillan, 2012), 161 (hereafter cited as *Sapphire's Literary Breakthrough*).

5. Fulton, "Looking for 'the Alternative[s],'" 161–62.

6. Elizabeth McNeil, "Deconstructing the 'Pedagogy of Abuse': Teaching Child Sexual Abuse Narratives," in *Sapphire's Literary Breakthrough*, 176.

7. L. H. Stallings, "Sapphire's *PUSH* for Erotic Literacy and Black Girl Sexual Agency," in *Sapphire's Literary Breakthrough*, 124, 125–26.

8. McNeil, "Deconstructing the 'Pedagogy of Abuse,'" 173, 176–77.

9. Lynette D. Myles, *Female Subjectivity in African American Women's Narratives of Enslavement: Beyond Borders* (New York/London: Palgrave Macmillan, 2009), 33.

10. Lucille Clifton, "*in the inner city*," 1969, in *The Collected Poems of Lucille Clifton*, ed. Kevin Young and Michael S. Glaser (Rochester, NY: BOA Editions Limited, 2012), lines 1 and 4.

11. Elizabeth McNeil, "Un-'Freak'ing Black Female Self: Grotesque-Erotic Agency and Ecofeminist Unity in Sapphire's *PUSH*," in *Sapphire's Literary Breakthrough*, 95.

12. Joni Adamson, "'Spiky Green Life': Environmental, Food, and Sexual Justice Themes in Sapphire's *PUSH*," in *Sapphire's Literary Breakthrough*, 70, 77.

13. Neal A. Lester, "'Rock the Motherfucking House': Guiding a Study of Sapphire's *PUSH*," in *Sapphire's Literary Breakthrough*, 183–84.

14. Ishmael Reed, "Fade to White," op-ed, *New York Times*, February 5, 2010, https://www.nytimes.com/2010/02/05/opinion/05reed.html.

15. Sapphire, letter to the editor, *New York Times*, February 11, 2010, https://www.nytimes.com/2010/02/12/opinion/l12sapphire.html.

16. Centers for Disease Control and Prevention website, cdc.gov, on October 21, 2020. When I returned in 2020 to the CDC website to verify statistics on African Americans and COVID-19, I couldn't find articles that had previously been published there. I learned, along with the rest of the American public, that many statistics on aspects of COVID-19 deaths and outcomes were removed from the website at the direction of the Trump administration.

penguin.co.uk/vintage